THE RESURRECTION WAGER

CHRISTOPHER COATES

Chapter 1

THE EARLY MORNING SUN HAD BEGUN TO SHINE THROUGH THE narrow gap in the faded, light blue curtains. Its illumination, still faint, revealed the sight of a spacious bedroom. A wood-framed, king-size waterbed was centered against the far wall, and various other pieces of oak bedroom furniture were in the room. All of this was sitting on a polished hardwood floor.

Most people would be ashamed of the condition of the room. Many of the dresser drawers hung wide open, their contents overflowing. Various items of clothing lay scattered about the floor. A few plates and glasses were on the floor next to the bed, and the nightstand had a half dozen brown glass bottles sitting on it. It appeared as if this was the bedroom of a sloppy and unsupervised teenager rather than that of a brilliant adult with a doctorate in quantum theory.

Eventually, the rumpled covers of the bed began to move as a man slowly struggled to a standing position. One could see him moving through the dim light as if he was ill or in considerable pain.

Paul Kingsman stood five foot ten and had a well-toned body and flat stomach. He was clean-shaven and tended to keep his hair short. He stumbled to the bathroom, which was located off the bedroom. His head pounded, and his vision was blurred. His mouth had a foul taste and was dry.

Eventually, Paul reached the bathroom and felt for the light switch. He knew he'd made a mistake as soon as he turned it on. The bright light greatly intensified the pounding in his head, and a muffled unhappy groan came from the bed behind him. Switching the lights back off, he stumbled forward in the dark, his night vision now gone.

Fumbling around in the dark, he worked by feel, found the faucet, and got the water running in the sink. He rubbed the cold water on his face several times using his hands. The water caused him to feel a little better. Next, he scooped a couple of handfuls of water to his lips and drank slowly, taking tiny sips. Paul knew better than to drink too much too quickly. Even the two small sips he'd already swallowed were beginning to churn his stomach.

Paul opened the medicine cabinet door and pulled out a small plastic bottle. In the near darkness, he couldn't read the printed label, but still shook four of the tablets into his hand and swallowed them. As they were going down, he briefly thought about how he hoped the pills had been the Ibuprofen he'd been planning on and not some of Michelle's Midol. He decided he didn't care and walked unsteadily back to the bedroom.

As he left the bathroom, Michelle brushed past him and, with a grunt of a greeting, shut the bathroom door.

Paul bumped the small nightstand as he returned to the bed and heard several empty glass bottles fall and hit the hardwood floor. Fortunately, it seemed as if none of them broke this time. He collapsed back on the bed and tried to lie as still as possible.

After several minutes the toilet flushed, and the sink started flowing. Paul distinctly heard the sound of the pills shaking around in the plastic bottle as Michelle fought with the childproof cap. Soon she was coming out of the bathroom, and he noticed she was wearing the blue, oversized, knee-length New England Patriots tee shirt that she frequently wore around the house.

When she dropped back down, the water in the mattress caused the whole bed to rock, and he moaned with discomfort as his head started pounding all over again.

"Sorry," Michelle said in a slightly slurred voice.

Paul grunted a reply that she understood meant he wasn't genuinely angered.

They lay still, not speaking for several minutes, then Michelle said with a hint of humor, "Do you think we'll ever learn?"

"It's not as much learning as remembering. Remembering how terrible the next morning feels."

"Are you still up to going today?" she asked.

Without hesitation, Paul answered, "Definitely, I'll be okay in a couple of hours, I just need some coffee and toast, and then I'll be as good as new. What about you?"

Michelle took a little longer to answer but finally agreed, "Let's not waste the day because we had a little too much to drink last night."

After several more minutes, they got up, and Michelle returned to the bathroom. This time she endured the bright light as she started the hot water in the shower.

Paul headed to the kitchen and got the container of coffee from the overhead cabinet; he scooped two spoonfuls into the filter compartment of the coffee maker, added water, and hit the power button.

While waiting, Paul went into the office, which was next to the living room, sat at the computer, and checked his email. While there, he also read the news and sports scores.

As he finished reading, the coffee maker beeped, indicating it was ready. He was finishing his first cup when Michelle came out of the bathroom.

"Coffee is ready," Paul told her as he headed to the shower.

Michelle poured hers and headed to the computer to conduct her own morning ritual that was similar to Paul's but lacked the sports scores.

By the time Paul's shower ended, she had dressed, and there was a plate of dry toast on the table in the kitchen.

Chapter 2

THIRTY-EIGHT-YEAR-OLD, PAUL KINGSMAN GREW UP AS AN only child in a single-parent home on the north side of Boston. His father, a firefighter with the Boston Fire Department, had developed brain cancer and died when Paul was only seven years old.

His mother, Emma Kingsman, worked hard to provide for her son. She worked long hours as a surgical nurse, she fought to balance the competing needs of her employment and being home for her son.

Even though he had a knack for getting into trouble, Paul excelled in school. During his high school years, he'd been arrested twice for minor juvenile offenses. Still, he managed to earn an academic scholarship to the University of Washington. While there, he completed his undergraduate and graduate studies in Quantum Mechanics. A few years later, he finished his doctoral studies at Berkley.

While at Berkley, Paul met Maureen Kraft, who was working on her Master's degree in Psychology. The two began dating, and two years later, they married and had two children, Heather and Adam.

During these years, Paul made some excellent investments

with extremely good payoffs. Several were so profitable and well-timed that an investigation by the Securities and Exchange Commission was started but never turned up anything inappropriate.

Paul's marriage only lasted four years before Maureen left him. She stated his work and education had so absorbed him that she needed something else.

Paul returned to Massachusetts and founded The Kingsman Research Institute. Paul's small fortune from his investments and various grants provided funding for the growing institute.

The Kingsman Research Institute primarily studied Quantum Mechanics and how the barrier between space and time worked.

A year ago, Paul sustained minor injuries to his back and shoulder. This injury resulted from a car driven by Michelle Rogers rear-ending him at a stop light near a shopping mall on the city's north side.

Michelle was a high school math teacher in Boston and was also recently divorced. She was a stocky woman who stood about five foot six inches. She had long brown hair, which she always wore pulled back.

After being married for six years, her doctor told Michelle and her husband Derek that she couldn't have children despite all they'd tried. Unfortunately, her eggs weren't healthy and couldn't be fertilized.

The doctors they followed up with gave them several options, including locating a surrogate egg donor or adoption. While this news crushed Michelle, her husband came up with another plan. He moved out of their home and filed for a divorce.

Eight weeks after finalizing the divorce, Michelle learned from a mutual friend that her ex-husband was an expectant father.

Following the traffic accident, Michelle and Paul began

dating. Their divorces had, however, changed their outlook on life. While still committed to his work, Paul took most weekends and evenings off, something he'd never have done before. He also had hired an assistant director of the institute who oversaw much of the ongoing research.

Michelle had also changed. While she once was quite conservative in dress and behavior, she'd become much more relaxed and sometimes almost reckless. This behavior change was one of the things Paul was most attracted to since it fit his personality very closely. He often had difficulty imagining her as she'd been. When she showed him photos of her previous self, Paul couldn't help feeling like he was looking at a completely different person.

They'd been living together for close to a year, and neither was in any hurry to try marriage again. However, they both thought it was only a matter of time.

Michelle had come to accept that she would never be a mother, and Paul, having two kids already, wasn't troubled by the idea.

Fortunately, Michelle was extremely fond of Heather and Adam and looked forward to the times when they came to visit almost as much as Paul did.

Chapter 3

MICHELLE AND PAUL WALKED OUT THE HOUSE'S SIDE DOOR and into the two-and-a-half-car-connected garage. The couple was dressed in denim shorts and had sandals on their feet. Michelle's blouse was all white, and she was carrying a large bag over her shoulder. She'd pulled her long brown hair back and held it in place with a clip.

Paul was wearing a red and black striped polo shirt and was pulling a wheeled blue cooler.

Even though the sunlight was not yet harsh, they both already had on their wrap-around sunglasses. Based on how her head still felt, Michelle assumed she'd probably wear them until she got into bed tonight.

Always being security conscious, Paul took his key and secured the deadbolt on the door. After climbing into the navy blue Ford SUV, Paul headed out of the driveway and turned to the left.

"How are you feeling?" Paul asked.

Michelle looked at him with an expression of disgust. "I feel terrible. I haven't felt like this in a couple of months. I need some more coffee. Do you mind stopping?"

"No problem. I could use some too. Do you have any more Ibuprofen in your bag, or should I get some?"

"Don't bother. I brought the whole bottle; you can have all you need."

"Good," Paul said with a nod of approval.

After several blocks, they pulled into a Mobil gas station, thankful that the usually busy station had several pumps available. After getting the fuel flowing, Paul went inside to get the drinks. Taking two 24oz cups, he added four pumps of cream to one, then filled both with coffee. When he'd paid for the fuel and coffee, Paul headed back to his vehicle. That's when he saw Tom Wallace walking confidently toward him.

Tom worked for Paul and served as the assistant director at The Kingsman Research Institute. Over the last few years, they'd become good friends.

Having studied together at the University of Washington, Paul was very impressed with Tom and his ability to beat technical problems down. Tom would work on an issue for as long as it took until he finally had it solved. He often came up with ideas Paul had never considered, and he was usually right. Paul considered him an invaluable asset and partner.

Unlike Paul, Tom didn't have his Ph.D. Instead, after completing his Master's degree, Tom concentrated his efforts more on working and the family he and his wife had started. Paul reluctantly had to agree Tom had made a better choice. Tom had three amazing kids, and Linda Wallace was a beautiful person, not just physically.

Tom indeed seemed to have the perfect family and marriage.

Paul was at times jealous when he thought about Tom's family situation. If he'd made better choices, he could have had the same thing. Instead, he had an ex-wife and two children that he only got to see about every other month because they lived on the opposite side of the country.

When Paul founded the institute, he hunted Tom down and found him working at a government-run research facility in central California.

Paul offered to double his salary if Tom agreed to come and work at the Kingsman Institute. When Tom finally accepted, Paul paid to move him and his family across the country.

Now, almost three years later, Paul was glad he'd gone to the expense and effort to bring Tom on board. Their research would never have progressed to the point where it had without Tom's involvement. Also, they'd become close friends.

"Hey, Tom. What are you up to this morning?" Paul asked.

As soon as he'd asked it, Paul knew he'd made a mistake. He knew where his friend was heading because Tom was dressed better today than he ever did at work, and it was Sunday.

"How are you doing, Paul? We're on our way to church, but I needed to get some gas first," Tom replied.

Paul nodded, "We're heading to the marina. We're going to spend the day on the boat. You should join us. We had a great time last month with you guys."

Tom replied, "We sure did have a good time. The kids are still talking about it. The weather is perfect, so I suspect you'll have a great day. But we can't go today. By the way, are you feeling okay? You don't look so good?"

Paul grinned, "We did a little too much partying last night, and now we're paying for it."

Tom nodded his understanding, "Why don't you and Michelle come with us? The marina and the nice weather will still be there in a few hours."

Paul chuckled, "You never give up. Do you?"

When Tom didn't reply immediately, Paul added, "Today is too nice a day to sit in church; I think we'll stick with the boat."

"Too bad, but make sure you don't get too much sun. Tomorrow's a very big day, and I don't want you to be unable to enjoy it because of a sunburn."

"Agreed, buddy. See ya tomorrow," Paul said as he climbed back into the SUV and handed Michelle her coffee, which she eagerly accepted.

Paul put the SUV in gear and pulled out of the service station, waving to Tom's family as he passed their Dodge sitting at the pump.

Michelle looked at Paul and smiled, "Was that Tom you were talking to? I heard something about going to church."

"Yeah, they're on their way there, and he invited us."

"Some people never give up. I know you've turned him down dozens of times," Michelle commented.

"True, but he isn't too annoying about it. He makes it clear where he stands and invites people to go. If you say no, he backs off. Tom's a good guy, and he means well."

"That's true; I like him too. I'd have said hi to Linda if I had realized it was them. What was he saying about tomorrow being a big day? I know I can't understand the details about what you do at the institute, but Tom made it sound like tomorrow is something special."

"It is," Paul explained. "Tomorrow, we'll try again to see if we can move something across the time barrier."

With excitement evident, Michelle responded, "That's amazing. Why didn't you tell me before?"

"I know most of the lab stuff isn't too interesting to you, and I try to leave work at work. Since we've tried and failed before, I didn't bother saying anything. But you're right. I should have at least mentioned it. If what we do works, it will be a really big deal."

As Paul said this, he pulled into the parking lot at the marina, and the conversation stopped.

They unloaded the SUV and headed to Paul's red and white power boat, which was named The Time Machine.

Within a few minutes, they'd cast off and soon glided out of the slip and headed into the bay.

Chapter 4

WHEN TOM WALLACE ARRIVED AT THE KINGSMAN RESEARCH Institute early the following day and was surprised to see so many other cars already in the parking lot.

The three-story building resided on twenty-five thickly wooded acres, about a half mile off the main road, and was invisible to anyone passing through the area. A river ran along the west edge of the property. It wasn't uncommon for those working there to see wildlife from their office windows. There were walking trails out back that some of the employees used at lunchtime.

Usually, the first to arrive, Tom found himself unconsciously grinning as he exited his vehicle and headed toward the entrance to the futuristic-looking building. Tom was glad that others on his staff were as excited as he was to begin today's experiments. Tom waved his ID badge in front of the scanner. He heard the audible buzzing as the door lock released to allow him access. In another half hour, these doors would unlock for the day.

While there was a reception desk, it was usually unoccupied. The location of the institute and the fact that this was a private facility meant there were few visitors. Anyone arriving could pick up the phone on the desk, and someone would come down to assist them.

Tom took the escalator up one floor, headed directly for his office, and hung his coat on the back of his door. He then placed his lunch in the small dormitory size refrigerator beside his desk.

Sitting at his desk, Tom forced the feeling of excitement down as he logged into his computer and opened his email.

Tom was working through the last of his messages when Paul burst into his office.

"Tom, I know you've your morning reading to do, but just for today, will you please delay it for a little while? Everyone's here, and we're desperate to see the recording. Now let's go!"

Paul turned and left the office.

Tom stood, smiled, and glanced down at the Bible on his desk. Spending some time meditating on the scriptures was essential to his morning. He felt the quiet study time always helped him prepare for the day. But he also had to admit that his excitement would diminish his ability to concentrate today. Since everyone was here early and ready to go, he'd feel guilty making them wait while he had his private time. Tom silently promised to read before lunch and then set off to meet with his team.

As Tom arrived, he heard the anxious chatter coming from those gathered. There was a sudden cheer as he entered the room.

Paul, who was at the front of the room, exclaimed, "Thanks for deciding to join us." The friendly laughter of everyone in the room drowned out Tom's response.

Tom sat at the head of the room next to Paul, who stood up and said, "Okay, the doors to the lab were locked over the weekend, and I'm the only one with the keys. The computer logs from the security system show that everyone did as I instructed this weekend. No one has attempted to enter this building since Friday afternoon. Also, the security doors at the lab stayed shut this weekend," Paul continued after a brief pause. "Therefore, we can safely say the experiment we did, or will do later this afternoon, was uncompromised," Paul waited as the excitement in the room grew. "Before we begin, I'm sure Tom has a few words for all of you."

Tom stood and surveyed the group and spoke, "I don't know if the experiment was successful, but if so," pausing for effect, Tom continued, "In just minutes, we might see the results of an experiment that we won't even conduct for several hours." This idea was nothing they all didn't already know, but just the concept of it made the room go silent as they all contemplated this fact again.

Tom sat back down, and Paul opened the video file on the computer beside him. The data resided on the server in the basement that held all the recorded security feeds. After several seconds, Paul called out to the room, "Here we go."

Moments later, the large LED screen mounted on the front wall lit up, and the image of the lab came into sharp focus. The time stamp, showing 1:01 AM Sunday, was visible in the lower right-hand corner. The picture was clear, and nothing was moving. There were workstations and various pieces of equipment visible in the background.

No one in the room was breathing as they stared intently at the LED screen. After almost a full minute, there was a collective gasp from the team. One second, everything looked the same as seconds before, and then instantly, there was a strange object in the middle of the room. It appeared like a rugged four-wheeled utility cart with several laptop computers hooked to it. There was a central piece of equipment with flashing lights and a digital screen.

At soon as the cart appeared, the motion-activated lights in the room came on, briefly corrupting the video until the camera adjusted.

Two identical video cameras were attached to the cart. The first was mounted on a short tripod and slowly rotated

360 degrees, revolving and filming the whole room. The other camera pointed directly at the screen of one of the two laptop computers. The cart-mounted instrument package sat still, recording while the top camera rotated for two complete revolutions, and then as suddenly as it appeared, it was gone.

The entire room exploded into applause. There was yelling and cheering. People were standing on chairs and exchanging high-fives with each other.

After several seconds, Paul stood and called out, "Okay, that's enough!" The mayhem decreased, and he continued, "Remember, people, you're congratulating yourselves for something you haven't even done yet." He continued, "We'll watch the tape again. Then we need to get to work. We still have to get Clyde tested, recharged, and send him back in time thirty-six hours."

Everyone retook their seats, and the recording played again. The team watched carefully, looking for any unexpected events they'd missed when first viewing the video.

Again they saw the cart, nicknamed Clyde, containing the instrument package, appear on the screen. Paul backed the recording up a couple of seconds. Then he ran it forward again, this time advancing it as slowly as possible. After about thirty seconds, they came upon the moment.

Clyde wasn't there, and one-tenth of a second later, he'd appeared. It was instantaneous. There was no flash of light or the image of it fading into focus. It was instantly there.

Chapter 5

CLYDE BEGAN HIS EXISTENCE AS A RUGGED-DUTY INDUSTRIAL equipment cart, which the team heavily modified. He had oversized pneumatic tires, which were about ten inches in diameter. The cart was four feet wide and five feet long and stood just over three feet tall. There was a flat surface on top. A metal box was sitting in the center of the surface, taking up most of it. It had numerous indicator lights and digital read-outs. The computers which held the data for the time jumps were contained within this box. Also in there was the secret technology that allowed Clyde to communicate with the actual time machine permanently located in the institute's basement, even when he traveled to a different time. A shelf below, just above the wheels, held four deep-cycle marine batteries. These provided all of Clyde's power when he wasn't plugged in.

While it was true, Clyde was the first to make the trip to the past and back successfully again; he wasn't the first to try.

When Paul first began working on the idea of moving something or someone back in time, there were many obstacles to overcome. He had always envisioned a standalone time ship to carry people from one time period to another.

As the research progressed, it became clear there were so

many serious problems with the plan that it became highly impractical. First, his time machine would need enormous amounts of power. It would need to have that energy available when it was in the past, where external electricity might not be possible. There were only a couple of ways to overcome these issues. One would require a massive diesel generator, making the time ship enormous and loud. That wasn't practical for slipping into a past time period and back unnoticed. The other option was a small nuclear reactor. While a reactor would be silent and more portable, Paul tried but couldn't get his hands on one for this project. The regulations and safety concerns would never allow it.

Paul knew he had to come up with a different approach. At the time when these challenges were being worked out, was when he brought Tom on board. Together they took the problem apart and realized the massive amount of energy and most of the hardware involved was for calculating the matrix and creating the portal to the past. Once they accomplished that goal, the team found the portal could be maintained as long as there was something on the other side to help hold it open.

Instead of sending the time machine to the past, it could remain in the present, open the portal, and send a small, low-power device through. Together the two machines would hold the gateway between time periods open, and the remote system could initiate the transit back at the given time. This change removed the need for a bulky, possibly loud device to travel to the past.

Because of this revelation, most of the early work centered on the device they built in the institute's basement. The team controlled it from the lab, and it did the heavy work of opening the portal to the past.

As this work progressed, Paul's engineers built the first remote system. It was an early version of Clyde and sat on a lab bench. The team nicknamed the device Mona.

No sooner was Mona created than the team noticed the problems. It wasn't portable and could never carry a person to the past. However, with the use of Mona and the systems in the basement, they were able to open a portal to the past. Unfortunately, they couldn't get a clear understanding of what time period it opened into.

This first success excited the team, and they reworked many processes, including rebuilding the device which would move through the portal. This time Paul and his team built the machine on a utility cart. It was far more portable than Mona and corrected many of her defects. This unit was named Wally. Early tests went better, and eventually, they decided it was time to send Wally back a day in time. Wally arrived at the correct time, but the location calculations needed refining. No one is sure of the exact location Wally arrived, but it was somewhere over the lab. It could have been one hundred feet in the air or a thousand. Either way, The 250-pound Wally crashed through the institute's roof and was found in pieces all over the spot where he departed from. On the night Wally made his historic jump, it was heavily raining, and water poured in through the gaping hole in the roof. The destruction of the device and damage to the work area of the lab set the efforts into time travel back eight months.

This setback didn't deter any of them because they'd succeeded in sending an object back in time, just not as planned. The project team pushed on working to refine the process and rebuild the remote device. This time they built a much more rugged machine. Four seats could be added or removed to allow multiple remote cameras or other equipment to be mounted. After much debate, this remote was named Clyde.

Chapter 6

EVERYONE SET OFF FOR THE LAB AFTER REPEATEDLY VIEWING and reviewing the recording. A lot of work remained to be completed before Clyde could make his historic but brief journey.

Tom, with the help of several technicians, began powering up Clyde. Over the next several minutes, the equipment that made up the time-traveling Clyde came to life. Power and computer cables ran from terminals built into the wall and connected to the various pieces of equipment on the cart.

Paul ran the final calibrations and tested the batteries to ensure they had a full charge. The video cameras were checked several times. No one wanted to repeat this work because of a misconfigured camera. After over an hour of preparation, Tom Wallace took a small remote control transmitter. He steered Clyde as he slowly rolled to the center of the room.

The laptop computer screen came to life. There was a video camera pointing directly at it, and it would record everything on the screen. That computer displayed the precise date and time down to the tenth of a second. There was a wireless network connection in the laptop, and it was getting the accurate time fed to it from a server in the basement of the building by way of an access point in the ceiling.

As soon as Clyde rolled into the center of the room, technicians removed most of the external cables, leaving only a single power and data connection.

"Begin the final calculation," instructed Tom.

"Yes, Mr. Wallace," answered Bruce Wilson. Bruce had been with the project for several months and was sitting at a terminal on the other side of the room today.

The servers in the institute's basement fed data to the equipment built into Clyde, and the massive calculations began. The data would enable the computers to calculate the quantum matrix and the journey to thirty-six hours in the past.

While this occurred, the onboard capacitors stored the needed power for the two intense bursts of energy. The first would send the unit back in time, and the second would allow it to return. After about forty-five minutes, there was an audible beep from Clyde.

"Processing complete," Tom called to the team.

"Initiate transit," Paul instructed.

Tom touched a button on a computer screen, and everyone in the room backed away from Clyde.

Several high-speed video cameras on tripods stood positioned about twenty feet from the small time machine. Each had a different view of the four-wheeled cart and its equipment. The recordings they were making now would provide a record of the event. The cameras would also carefully watch the moment Clyde made during his jump and return to see if they could learn anything more.

The camera mounted on top of Clyde began to rotate, and seconds later, there was a brief buzzing sound, and the power and data cables ejected themselves from the equipment on the cart.

Clyde now stood free. There was minimal noise coming

from him and the camera, which was turning, but there appeared to be nothing else going on. Tom started the count-down from five. When he got to zero, Clyde instantly disappeared.

They expected this, but most still gasped when it happened.

Less than three seconds later, Clyde was back and looked as if he'd never left.

Charlie Baker, a new technician to the project, reattached the data cable but left the power disconnected. At the same time, Tom started entering commands into his computer keyboard. The camera stopped revolving, and various systems began powering off.

As soon as Tom downloaded all the data the various sensors had collected during the brief trip, he used the remote to move Clyde out of the center of the room and then powered the remaining systems off.

Bruce Wilson disappeared to review the data obtained by the onboard sensors. The rest of the team returned to the conference room.

This time, instead of watching something enter the room from a different time period, they'd be observing the actual passage from one point in time to another.

The first recording came to life, and they saw the image of the lab. As the camera rotated, they saw several rotations where everyone was visible and staring at the revolving camera and the equipment package under it.

The background voices were barely audible, and then Tom's came from the speakers as he counted backward from five down to one. There was the slightest distortion in the recording. It was so brief that they almost didn't notice it, and then the picture was clear again. However, as the camera rotated, there were several noticeable differences. The room was darker, and the computer data and power cables, which had been visible lying on the floor when the camera faced east, weren't there. Also, no people were watching. Seconds later, the image brightened as the lights in the lab came on. After about fifteen seconds, the momentary distortion returned, and the whole team was again visible in the image.

The second video showed the view of the laptop computer's screen. The time on the screen was exact, and the laptop synchronized its time from the server twice each second. The image the staff watched on the LED display jumped once and was instantly clear again. Two more tenths of seconds passed, and the time on the laptop screen stopped momentarily, and then the time and date jumped thirty-six hours in the past. The laptop then began counting time normally for almost fifteen seconds, and then the picture jumped again. In less than a second, the computer time had returned to the current time.

As the recording finished, the conversations began slowly and then increased in intensity. The primary topic of discussion was how the instrument package had left for the past and returned in three seconds. However, there was proof it had spent a full fifteen seconds in the past.

That appeared to mean Clyde was now twelve seconds older than he should be. This was something they hadn't considered. More interesting was the question, how significant was this? Also, what implications did it hold? Could they have changed the timing to have Clyde return before he even left? The opportunities for additional experimentation seemed endless.

As they discussed these concepts, Bruce entered the room and handed Paul a tablet with the latest test results on the screen. Paul read the screen quickly and then gave it to Tom.

Tom took the device and viewed the list of factors on the screen. Smiling, he handed it back to Paul, who stood again and said, "Okay, people, quiet down."

The silence was immediate. "We now have the preliminary report based on the data Clyde collected on his journey. We've all been curious as to how the effects of a jump through time might affect a person," Paul paused and looked out over his staff.

The sensors were calibrated to take readings thousands of times per second. They did this to tell what forces acted upon the object passing through time. It was critical to know if those forces would be harmful to people.

"From what the data shows, the total time it took to make the time jump was almost instantaneous, less than one, one-thousandth of a second. There was no increase or decrease in atmospheric pressure detected. Radiation levels were lower during the jump than the standard background radiation we all experience daily. The temperature increased slightly, but only a few degrees. That's probably from the friction of moving through the quantum barrier. There nothing to suggest there's any danger in sending a person on this journey."

OVER THE NEXT FOUR WEEKS, the experiment was repeated several times with multiple variations. In one of the final tests, a young gray and white cat named Willard was placed in a pet carrier. Tom strapped the carrier to the top of Clyde and sent it back thirty days. After spending fifteen minutes in the past, Clyde returned the cat to the present time.

Willard was tested and watched for a week and continued to show no ill effects from his adventure.

The excitement from the success of the tests continued to grow, and there were many suggestions for additional experiments to conduct. Also, debate began growing about what to do with this new technology.

Chapter 7

THE SUN WAS STARTING TO RISE EARLY ON MONDAY MORNING when Paul Kingsman left his home and headed for work. It was almost a full hour earlier than he usually departed. However, he knew Tom Wallace was an early bird and he wanted an uninterrupted conversation with him. Paul wanted to discuss the subsequent testing phases before the facility got busy.

Paul entered the front doors and took the escalator to the second floor. He dropped his jacket and laptop case off in his office and headed down the hall to see if Tom was at his desk.

As he stepped into Tom's office, his eyes were, as always, drawn to the large, framed picture on the wall directly opposite the door. It was of Jesus and showed him wearing a crown of thorns. His hands were reaching out, and the nail holes were visible. At the bottom of the picture, it said: "I am the way and the truth and the life. No one comes to the Father except through me. John 14:6."

Something about the look on Jesus' face always caught Paul's attention. It was a look of kindness and something more that Paul couldn't place words on. He knew it was just an artist's rendition of what Jesus might have looked like, but it still caught his attention every time.

It bothered Paul how the picture affected him. Paul wasn't a religious person. He'd attended Sunday school as a child but had lost interest in religion as he got older. Instead, he preferred to find scientific explanations for the world's mysteries.

Even if he didn't understand its appeal, Paul respected Tom's dedication to his faith. That respect was why he'd never asked Tom to move the picture to a less prominent place in his office. It was also why Paul was willing to occasionally listen politely as Tom spoke about his faith and of Jesus.

But Paul also had to laugh when he thought about all the effort Tom had spent trying to interest him in God. And how completely unsuccessful he'd been.

There was still the fact that Tom Wallace didn't just speak of his beliefs but lived what he believed. This last part almost made Paul listen to what Tom said a little more closely.

This morning, as usual, Tom was seated at his desk; he was closing his bible as Paul walked in.

"Morning Tom."

Tom looked up and, without thinking about it, glanced at the clock on his desk. As he did so, he said, "Hey. What are you doing here so early?"

"I wanted to discuss our next steps. Since things tend to get busy around here, I figured we could discuss it before everyone arrives. Unless you're in the middle of something," Paul explained.

Tom smiled. He always appreciated Paul respecting the personal time he took each morning, even if he didn't understand it. "I just finished reading, so this is an excellent time."

Paul shut the door to the spacious office, pulled up a chair, and sat across from his friend.

"So, what are your thoughts?" Tom asked.

Paul paused briefly and then began, "The way I see it, there are still two big things we need to test."

Tom nodded and added, "Sending a person back."

"Correct and testing to see if it is possible to make a change to something that has happened in the past. There's been lots of debate about whether it'll even be possible to make a change," Paul continued.

"Agreed, but there are risks to changing the past."

"Absolutely, but in a controlled setting, making a specially planned change will pose no risk if we handle it carefully. I believe proving whether or not we can change the past is a necessary step in determining what we'll do with this technology," Paul explained.

"Ok, I buy that. But we've got to be sure any change we make has a measurable outcome."

"Exactly," Paul responded.

"I take it you have something in mind?"

"It is rough, and we'll need to clean up the details a bit, but I want to rig up a device in the lab. Maybe, something as simple as a mechanical trapdoor on a timer. We set the timer for one AM, and at that time, the trapdoor opens, and a light bulb or some other fragile object falls through to the floor, where it breaks. We'll come in the next day and see the broken pieces. We then send someone back to two hours before the bulb was due to fall, and they prevent it from happening," Paul explained.

Tom thought about the idea for a minute and, with a nod, said, "That makes sense. This experiment won't be too hard to set up. I can get everything in place in a few hours. Let's do this tonight."

"Perfect."

"I assume you're going to want to make the first trip?" Tom asked with mild disappointment in his voice.

"This one is mine," Paul confirmed. "The next one is all yours."

Chapter 8

Bruce Wilson grabbed his lightweight gray jacket and put it on as he walked. He headed down the back stairs of the Institute toward the walking trails. Many employees liked to walk these paths at lunch when the weather was pleasant. Today the sun was trying to push through the thick clouds. It was supposed to rain, but Bruce hoped it would hold off until after dinner because he'd two nice racks of ribs he was planning to grill when he got home.

Bruce was concerned he might not have this chance to walk today because of all the excitement surrounding the upcoming round of additional experiments. He knew he should've passed on his walk and worked through lunch, but this always helped clear his mind. Bruce decided to walk the half loop and head back instead of going the entire distance, which would take forty-five minutes to complete.

As he headed for the trail, he heard someone coming up from behind. Stopping, he peered back and saw Charlie Baker.

Charlie had just started at the Institute about a month before. He seemed like a nice guy, and the two of them had walked at lunch several times and were becoming friends.

"Thanks for waiting for me," Charlie said.

"No problem. I'm keeping it short today. I've got too much to do."

"Yeah, I know. I need to run another systems calibration test," Charlie explained.

The two men walked silently for a few minutes, then Charlie said, "Have you ever thought about all the things we could do with this technology?"

"Sure, we're always looking for how to prove it and show the world its potential," Bruce explained.

"No. I mean, personally. If I could go back and tell myself to invest everything in Microsoft or Google, or maybe buy dirt cheap Apple stock, I'd be rich overnight." Charlie theorized.

"Sure, we all think like that. Great bets could be placed if we could communicate back to the past who the Super Bowl winner would be or which horse would win the Kentucky Derby. But while it's fun to think like those things, don't let Paul hear you say it out loud. He's extremely concerned about keeping the reputation of the work at the Institute clean," said Bruce.

"I know. I don't say anything in the office. But it wouldn't be tough to do, would it? How would anyone ever know? The change would be the new reality."

Bruce paused briefly before answering, "No, it wouldn't be difficult. But you're talking like you might actually try to do something. There are too many things to factor in. Running the calculations isn't as easy as it looks. I suggest you stop thinking so much about this. It'll only lead to trouble."

"Yeah, I guess so. But it's fun to fantasize about it."

"That it is," Bruce agreed.

The two of them made the last turn and headed back. Both were lost in their own thoughts. Each of them was thinking similarly dangerous things.

Chapter 9

EARLY THE FOLLOWING DAY, PAUL WALKED INTO THE LAB. ON the floor was a shattered light bulb. Bending down, he up the bulb's base with the jagged glass edges sticking out. He carefully turned it over in his hand while absently thinking about what would happen in a few hours. He would travel back about twelve hours to remove this light bulb from Tom's contraption and place it on the counter so it wouldn't be damaged.

"I see it broke," said the voice from behind him.

Startled, Paul whipped around and saw Tom standing in the doorway. As he turned, his hand jerked, and one of the glass edges of the destroyed light bulb ripped into the side of the index finger on his right hand. Paul gave out a small yelp as the blood started dripping.

"Sorry, Paul. I thought you heard me walk up," Tom said as he hurried forward to check his friend's hand.

There was a half-inch laceration. The wound wasn't deep enough to require stitches but was actively bleeding.

"Not your fault. I was lost in thought and didn't hear you."

As they spoke, Tom walked to the row of cabinets on the west wall and explored three before locating and with-

30

drawing a first aid kit. With just a few minutes of effort, Tom stopped the bleeding and wrapped the finger with a bandage.

"Thanks for fixing me up," Paul said. "However, using a computer keyboard for a few days will be hard."

"If you're successful with the test today, maybe your injury will never have happened because the light bulb will never break."

"That's right. I hadn't thought about it." Paul said with a smile.

TWO HOURS LATER, Paul worked the remote control unit and wheeled Clyde back to the center of the lab. Today would be the fifth time jump for Clyde, who looked slightly different than he had on his previous trips.

The laptop computer, which tracked time and date, and the video camera to monitor it were removed.

Instead of being on a revolving tripod, the second camera was on an extendable arm. The onboard computer which ran Clyde's systems also controlled the camera. It was programmed to follow all of Paul's movements, ensuring he was always in the center of the frame.

There was a simple metal seat attached to the cart. Also, there were several buttons on a small control panel.

Technicians spent twenty minutes reviewing all of Clyde's systems, ensuring everything was in order. All the while, the data and power connectors were attached and transferring information and energy.

Tom was conversing with the technicians, and after several minutes, he walked to Paul, who was nervously pacing. "The route's been calculated, and everything is ready."

"Then I guess it's time to go," Paul said excitedly, hoping his nervousness didn't show as he took his seat on Clyde.

Paul looked around and saw his entire team standing

around, staring at him as he sat on a small seat that was bolted to the utility cart, and he felt more than a little foolish.

Not knowing what a time traveler might experience, a simple seatbelt with a plastic clasp was attached to the seat, and Paul clipped it in place. After a brief pause, he took a deep breath and said, "Here it goes." And with that, he pressed a button on the console marked "1".

Immediately the power and data cables ejected from the equipment on the cart. Paul heard many voices yelling, "Good luck," "Be careful," and other similar words of encouragement. Still, he focused on the computer voice, which had started counting down. When it reached zero, Paul felt a brief shiver and a warm sensation. Looking around, he realized the lab was not as brightly lit, and all his staff was gone.

Climbing off Clyde caused the motion-activated lights to kick on.

On the main work table was Tom's contraption, with the intact light bulb lying on the trap door waiting to fall. Paul went to it, removed it from the device, and placed it in a bowl to ensure it didn't roll off the table and break.

As his eyes swept the room, they came across Clyde backed into the corner, where he usually sat. Paul looked at him for a moment, then turned around and looked at the center of the room, and Clyde was sitting there too. The telescoping arm held the video camera and was following his every movement.

There was something eerie about seeing the same equipment cart sitting in two different places in the room at the same time.

After several more seconds of looking around, Paul returned to the center of the room, climbed onto Clyde, and pressed the button marked "2". Again there was a warm sensation accompanied by a slight shiver, and he was aware the room was bright, and there were people all around him.

The cheering began, and Paul threw a triumphant wave

with his right hand. There was still a bandage and laceration on his index finger, but only Paul knew why it was there. Because in everyone else's reality, his finger had never been injured.

Charlie Baker began downloading data from Clyde's computers when Paul got up from the seat.

Paul underwent a brief medical examination. The team checked his blood pressure and heart rate, and EKG. A team member drew some blood and would send it out for testing and comparison to a previously drawn sample. After the examination, Tom and Paul disappeared into Paul's office.

A flow chart on the whiteboard diagrammed a slightly modified version of the plan Tom had proposed the previous day.

"I don't know about you, Paul," Tom began, "I know we succeeded in proving what we wanted, but I've trouble feeling like we did anything. I know that when we left the office last night, the light bulb was in the contraption and ready to fall," Tom said, pointing to the flowchart.

"But I fully recall going back and stopping the bulb from falling. I also remember the broken bulb this morning. I even sliced my finger on it and have the cut to prove it. Even though I prevented it, since I'm the one who went back and made the change, the memories stayed with me when I returned after making the change," Paul stated.

"That means you and I are living with different realities because when I came into work this morning, the bulb had never broke," Tom continued.

"This is all quite interesting," Paul finished.

Tom smiled and nodded, "It hurts to try to think it through, but we know you succeeded in both of our efforts. You went back in time and changed the outcome of a specific event."

"I guess the next step is to figure out where we go from here," Paul stated.

"One thing we should begin working on is redesigning the equipment. Say we want to send someone back to witness or intervene in a specific event in the Revolutionary War. I think showing up on the ridiculous-looking equipment cart would be a problem," Tom explained.

Paul nodded and laughed, "Millions of dollars went into building Clyde, and you call him ridiculous looking?"

Tom smiled, but before he could speak, Paul added, "I agree. Are you thinking of a more portable device?"

"Yes, probably some sort of backpack unit. We'll need it sooner or later, and it'll give everyone something to work on while we discuss where we go from here."

Chapter 10

AT TWO IN THE MORNING, THE PARKING LOT WAS DARK. THE tall lights had shut off automatically an hour earlier, and the headlights of the approaching vehicle briefly lit the lot. The illumination only lasted momentarily, as the driver shut the car's lights off as he entered the parking area. With sixty to choose from, Bruce Wilson picked a spot heavily shaded by some trees. Hopefully, the security cameras would have their view of this space partially blocked.

The small, older Ford Focus stopped, and Bruce slipped on a black ski mask and put on a ball cap with a Red Sox logo to hide his face. He'd borrowed the car from a friend and picked up the cap at a thrift store earlier in the afternoon.

Bruce had explained to his friend that his pickup truck was having problems and that he needed to use the Focus tonight. In truth, there was nothing wrong with his truck. But Bruce didn't want his vehicle visible on the security video. The truck was distinct, and anyone might recognize it.

Tonight's mission wasn't something Bruce had felt ready to do. Still, his recent conversation with Charlie Baker had forced him to get this done immediately. He was concerned

Charlie would do something foolish, and security and building access would become tighter.

Approaching the front door, he pulled a generic access card from his pocket. This card had been the most challenging part of his plan. The security team programmed the cards on-site, and it took him three days to find an opportunity to get into the IT area. He needed to find a time when the two guys who worked in the department were at lunch. It had taken some work to figure out how to program a new card with the needed access. Now he'd find out if it had worked. With sweaty palms, he swiped the access card, the door clicked, and he pulled it open. The only question remaining was, would it work to get into the lab?

Bruce walked quickly and confidently through the lobby and the halls, heading for the lab. There were too many security cameras to avoid them all. Ignoring them, he ducked his face and headed toward his objective.

The forged access card worked again; he was now in the lab. He turned off the motion sensor because he didn't want the overhead lights coming on, which someone outside might see.

Working in the reduced light, with a strap-on headlamp, he went to the computer terminal and took twenty minutes to type in all the data.

While it was processing, he moved Clyde into the center of the room and hooked up the power and data connections. After waiting another fifteen minutes, the computer indicated it was ready. After disconnecting the data connection, Bruce climbed up onto the seat. Next, he attached the seatbelt and pressed the button marked "1". There was a brief warm sensation and then nothing.

Climbing off the cart, he walked to the counter. The date on the computer was eight days in the past. Bruce left the lab and crossed the hall to his cubicle. He withdrew a small piece of paper from his pocket, opened the desk drawer, and placed the paper inside. The note was folded in half, with a date and long series of numbers written on it. Next, he took the stapler off his desk and sat it on his chair, and pushed the chair under the desk. That would be the signal to make sure he looked into the desk drawer. Making his way back to the lab, he felt relieved at how easy this had been.

Currently, he was up to his ears in debt and was two months behind on his mortgage. Most of the debt came from several years ago when his wife underwent a full year of treatments for breast cancer. At that time, he wasn't working at Kingsman, and his family had no medical insurance. Soon after he returned to his time, he'd have one hundred and sixteen million dollars, and he and his now healthy wife could relax.

Tomorrow he'd resign his position at Kingsman. Sitting on the cart, he pressed the button marked "2". He felt the same sensation and was back in his own time. He spent the next fifteen minutes putting all the equipment back precisely as he'd found it and worked to delete the data related to tonight's unauthorized work from the computer.

Chapter 11

OVER THE NEXT FEW MONTHS, THE STAFF WORKED TO CLEAN up the design of the time-traveling cart and condense it into a more portable device. During those months, Tom and Paul met several times, trying to determine the project's next phase.

Paul had worked for many years to get to where they were now. Having reached it, he didn't know what to do with this technology. The more they discussed it, the more doubt there was that this capability was something they should make public. The ability to change the past sounded great at first. However, the more he thought about the implications of what this could mean, the more frightening their discovery seemed.

These issues sparked many debates among the staff. One person suggested that technology should be used to go back and prevent Adolf Hitler from coming to power. Someone else suggested they should stop the assassination of President Kennedy from happening. Many others wanted to go back a few weeks and provide their past selves with the winning lottery results from a massive jackpot recently paid out. One of the team, Pam, had a brother who was killed by a drunk driver ten years before. She wanted to go back and prevent his death from occurring.

As the team debated, it became clear that while all of these suggestions sounded good initially, they were all terrible ideas.

If Hitler had never come to power, it was correct many innocent deaths could have been prevented. However, if all those people had survived, they'd have gone on to marry and have families. Some of them would undoubtedly have married people who had gone on to connect with different people.

Many children who had been born would never have been. Different children would have been born instead. Over the years, this would completely reshuffle tens of millions of lives and families. Some people currently on the team might have never been conceived.

Also, if they prevented Hitler from conducting his actions against the Jews, the post-war nations who worked to form the modern country of Israel would've had no reason to do such a thing. That modern-day country might not exist, and the entire Arab situation would be completely different. The whole world would be affected, in some ways for the better, but some, certainly for the worse.

Preventing Kennedy's assassination would possibly cause monumental changes in our nation's current political appearance.

Even preventing Pam's brother's death would result in loss of life. At the time of his death, he'd recently gotten married and had no children. Since his death, his wife had remarried, and she and her husband had a son and a pair of twin daughters. Those children would never have been born if Pam's brother had survived.

The only thing suggested that no one could see potential damage coming from was returning in time and providing yourself the past with the winning lottery ticket numbers from a few weeks before. However, the news of this project would eventually become public. If it became known the team had been tampering with time for personal gain, the credibility of their work would be suspect. Ethical questions about this technology's existence would overshadow its enormous potential.

Tom was in his office reviewing test data when Paul stepped in and said, "Mind if I come in for a moment?"

Tom looked up and saw a sly, almost mischievous look on Paul's face. "Of course not," Tom answered. "What's on your mind?"

With that look on Paul's face, Tom suspected this would be interesting.

As Paul entered, the picture of Jesus hanging above Tom's desk drew his attention. Paul felt his grin broaden slightly. Paul closed the door and dropped into a seat.

"I think I have an answer," Paul began.

"Good. An answer to what?" Tom continued.

"An answer to what we can do as the next step of testing this technology. In fact, after this, I think we'll begin trying to determine how we'll publicize our work."

"Oh really, please share the secret!" Tom said eagerly.

"We've already determined that going back and changing anything except the immediate past could have disastrous complications we can't even predict," Paul continued.

"Exactly."

"So I started thinking, what can you do with this technology besides changing the past? Finally, I came up with something," Paul said and then paused.

Tom looked at him impatiently, "Well, spill it!"

Paul laughed slightly and continued, "We use this technology to return and study the past, ensuring we don't accidentally change the course of events."

Tom waited for him to continue, unsure where this was going. So far, this wasn't very exciting.

Paul saw his explanation hadn't completely taken hold. "There are mysteries that society has been studying for years and still have no answer to. You see, we don't prevent the assassination of President Kennedy; we could send historians back and observe and document it and find out what really happened. Or another option, think how much easier it would be if archaeologists could go back and view the ancient civilization before excavating its current site."

By this point, Tom was nodding his understanding, and Paul relaxed a bit, seeing things were sinking in.

"Now for the exciting part. Before we make this public, we go back in time and answer and document one of the most hotly debated topics of all time," Paul explained.

"What topic is that?" Tom asked.

Paul's grin was now ear-to-ear at his friend's question; it was the one he needed Tom to ask. Before Paul answered, he theatrically pointed to the wall just above and behind Tom's head.

As Tom turned and looked at the picture on the wall, Paul answered, "We go and find out if He really was the Son of God."

At this, Tom whipped his head back around and stared at Paul with a complete look of shock on his face.

Chapter 12

TOM COULD FEEL THE COLOR DRAIN OUT OF HIS FACE WHEN
Paul made his suggestion. For several moments he sat there
staring at the mischievous grin on his friend's face. This was
the most absurd thing he'd ever heard.

After getting over the initial shock, he began to feel a little
excited about the proposal as he started thinking about it.

Not only was this an opportunity to see Christ in person,
but it was the opportunity to prove to millions that Christ was
the true Son of God.

Tom had often fantasized about meeting the Lord. Now
there was the opportunity actually to go back and see him in
person. It seemed ridiculous and fantastic all at the same time.

"What do you have in mind, Paul?" Tom asked.

"Well, I was thinking about the best way to demonstrate
this technology, and I got this idea. How about a little wager
between the two of us? If we go back and prove Jesus was a
great prophet and teacher, but nothing more, you take down
your picture and personally write up the findings. Including
the proof that Christ wasn't divine," Paul said with a grin.

"And what happens when we prove he is the Son of God?"
Tom inquired.

"If that happens, we'll have proof, and I'll make certain not just to document it when we go public but I'll start going to church with you on Sundays."

Tom was amazed at the opportunity which had suddenly become available to him. Not just the chance to meet Christ, but he'd finally get Paul to go to church with him.

Before he had time to consider the implications of the wager, Tom said, "You have a deal."

"Excellent!" Paul while holding out his hand, which Tom shook.

"So, do you have a plan for how this will go down?" Tom asked.

"Just the early stages of one," Paul began. "We'll have to complete the backpack units and arrive in that time period at an agreed upon point. Next, we'll have to record specific occurrences without detection and then return home."

"This is going to take a lot of preparation; we'll have to obtain native dress, learn the area, and determine good lookout points, all before going back. Not to mention, they didn't speak English in that region, and we must be certain not to change history," Tom added.

"Now you see why I'm so excited," Paul said. "This isn't just about going back a day or two in a lab. This will involve interacting with a culture from two thousand years ago. All the while making sure we prevent our identity from being known. It'll be the adventure of a lifetime."

"Linda has a friend at work, Jeff Collins. His wife is a professor at Boston University. She teaches history and specializes in that period. We've had dinner a few times, and I bet if I give her a call, we might be able to interest her in doing some consulting to prepare us for this."

"Can you call her now?" Paul asked excitedly.

"She works most days, but I can leave her a message to call my cell."

"Excellent, tell her we'll pay her fifty dollars an hour for her time," Paul said.

Paul stood and paced the room as Tom made the phone call and left the message.

After Tom hung up, he said, "If she isn't interested, I'll have her give me the name of someone who might be. I wouldn't be surprised if she knew other professors with a background in this area. I know she attends several conferences each year, so she must have some contacts."

"Sounds good to me. We should be able to get somebody to work with us," Paul said.

"What else do you think we'll need to do to prepare for this?" Tom asked.

"I don't know, but we should think about it and make a list of anything that comes to mind," Paul responded. Then after a moment, he added. "I guess we should determine how we're going to accomplish this. What will it take to prove or disprove that He is the Son of God? What do we look for? I don't think just walking up to him and asking will be the best approach."

Tom briefly thought about this question and said, "That's easy. There's historical proof Christ lived. Even non-believers recognize him as a great teacher. So while I'd love to listen to him teach, that would prove nothing. Even some of the miracles he performed could be explained away by skeptics, such as yourself," Tom grinned, and Paul nodded.

Tom added, "But there's one clear way to prove or disprove his deity."

"What, witness his death on the cross? I'm not sure that would convince me. Many people were crucified back in those days," Paul asked.

"No, not his death; everyone dies—his resurrection. Christ's resurrection is the one event that makes it clear he was much more than a great teacher and prophet. He fulfilled Old Testament promises recorded over a thousand years earlier by coming out of the tomb three days after his death. With that one act, he verified he was the Son of God.

"I read a book once which said that if anyone ever wanted to destroy Christianity, the only thing they had to do, was disprove the resurrection. If we watch the tomb and someone steals the body before the third day, it is all a big lie. But if he walks out of the tomb on his own, his diety is proven."

"So you're saying all we've got to do is get there and see if he comes out of the tomb? That isn't too difficult," Paul said.

"There is a little more to it than that. No one knows for sure exactly where the tomb is. We'll have to locate it. Also, if we show Jesus coming out of the tomb, there will still be some skeptics who won't believe. I want to anticipate their arguments so we have the proof needed to refute them."

"Ok, I'll buy that," Paul said. "We'll write down anything else which comes to mind and then go over everything we come up with. In the meantime, I want to talk to the fabrication guys. We need to determine how big and heavy these backpack units will be and how much battery consumption we'll experience there. We need to know how long we'll be able to spend in the past. For the systems to maintain the path back to our time, we'll need to keep the units operational at all times. That means a constant power drain in a society that's eighteen hundred years away from understanding electricity."

"Quite right," Tom agreed. "This isn't a journey we'll be taking very soon. There's going to be considerable planning and preparation involved. We're going to need it to document all the things we'll have to prepare for. We'll also want all our planning documented so we can combine it with the documentation we eventually release after this is complete."

"Ok, it sounds like we've got a good start going. Let me know if the professor agrees to meet and when she'll be here. I'm going to get going; I want to get to the lab before the team breaks up for the day."

As Paul got up to leave, Tom spoke again. "One last thing I want to run past you."

Paul turned back but didn't retake his seat.

"I was thinking; we need a way to communicate to ourselves in the past in case of an emergency."

Tom could see Paul wasn't following him by the perplexed look on his face.

"Think of it this way, say you go back in time on an experiment, and something goes wrong. Maybe a calculation error, equipment failure, or anything. After determining what the problem was, I would have to go back in time to prevent the incident from occurring. We need a way to communicate with our past selves to convey there's a crisis related to time travel, and any instructions left must be precisely followed."

"I like that. We need a code to tell us there's such an emergency, one specific to a change in the past going wrong," Paul paused and added, "Something like a quantum crisis."

"Quantum crisis? Wow, that's kinda dorky. How about just QC for short?" Tom asked.

"Ok, I guess QC sounds better. If there isn't anything else, I'll be in the lab, have a good night."

"You too, Paul."

Chapter 13

CATHERINE COLLINS WAS TIRED. IT HAD BEEN A LONG DAY, finishing up an even longer week. Now here she was, giving up her Friday evening to meet some geeks about a consulting project. She was only considering this work because she and her husband had just remodeled their house. During the project, they spent more than double what they'd budgeted.

Then as she thought about it, she had to admit that since it was Tom Wallace who'd called, she probably would have still met with him, but probably not on a Friday evening. She'd met Tom and Linda on several occasions, they were both great people, and Tom was more than a little attractive.

She navigated the new black Volvo into the parking lot, which belonged to the Kingsman Institute, and was surprised. This facility was tucked away and out of sight. She would never have suspected such an impressive-looking building was located right on the outskirts of the city. She suspected few people even knew it was here.

There were only three other vehicles in the parking lot, so she pulled up close to the door and, out of habit, made sure she was parked directly under one of the light poles. It wasn't dark yet, but if this meeting went on for more than an hour, it would be when she returned to her car.

She stepped from the vehicle and clicked the button on the keychain remote, which locked all the doors as she walked to the building.

As she climbed the steps and approached the doors, Tom Wallace held the door open for her, and with a genuine smile, she stepped into the lobby.

"Catherine, I'm glad you made it. Did you have any trouble finding us?" Tom asked.

"No, not at all, the directions were fine, and I'm somewhat familiar with the area. But I didn't know such a modern building like this was located here in town."

"I know. Paul, our director, picked this location so we'd be close but also out of the way and, more to the point, out of view."

As Tom relocked the door, Catherine looked around and continued her questioning. "What's it you guys at the Kingsman Institute do?"

"Paul Kingsman founded the institute several years ago to study quantum mechanics and to try to develop practical applications for the theories surrounding that field," Tom explained as he headed for the escalator, which led up a level.

Catherine followed right behind, still asking questions. "So you guys are physicists?"

"Exactly."

"Are you sure you understand my field of study?"

Tom withheld a small laugh as he answered, "You're a historian specializing in the Middle East. You specifically focus on the events of about two thousand years ago. I also believe you're well versed in the languages and dialects of that time."

"Good. I was afraid there was some confusion as to my area of expertise. What would a bunch of physicists need consulting from a historian for?" Catherine asked.

Instead of answering, Tom said, "We're in here," and

directed her to a conference room. The room had an oval table in the center with about a dozen chairs surrounding it. On the table were two laptop computers. One was connected to a large LED monitor on the wall. There was also a USB flash drive with a piece of paper wrapped around it sitting on the table, along with a manila folder and an assortment of pens and markers.

Paul looked up from his laptop and smiled at her.

"Professor Collins, I'm Dr. Paul Kingsman, the director of this facility. Please call me Paul." As they shook hands, Paul continued. "Tom has told me about your credentials. He suggests you might be the right person to provide some consultation for a project we've got going on here."

"Thanks for inviting me. I'm just a little confused about what my expertise can do for you," Catherine said.

"I understand. However, before we get to that, I must get your signature on a confidentiality agreement," Paul said, sliding a four-page document to her. He added, "We don't currently do any classified government work, but the nature of our project insists on absolute secrecy at this time."

As Catherine studied the document, she was starting to feel a little uneasy about what she was getting involved in. However, her curiosity was peaked, and the only way she'd ever know what this was about was to sign the document.

While skimming through it, Catherine noticed the statements promising legal recourse should she disclose to anyone the nature of the work conducted at the Kingsman Institute. After brief consideration, she scooped the pen off the table and signed the documents.

"Excellent," Paul began. "We have a little presentation for you that will hopefully explain what we're doing and what we'd like to hire you to provide."

Tom turned down the lights and a video presentation began. It contained an elementary explanation of quantum theory. Then Paul continued with a description of their work at the Kingsman Institute. "We have been working on creating a process to allow us, for lack of a better description, to navigate through the space-time barrier into another point in time. Once we can navigate to a specific time and place, our equipment has no difficulty transporting us to that point in time."

Catherine's expression was incredulous. "You mean to say you're working on traveling back in time? You have a vehicle that travels back in time?" There was a definite tone of doubt in her voice.

"That is more or less what we've done," Tom explained.

"Well, you must excuse me if I seem a bit doubtful, but what you're describing seems completely amazing."

"I know. We have been working on this project for a long time, and it still seems a bit absurd to us, too," Tom said.

"I want to show you something else," Paul added.

Pressing a series of keys on the laptop, the first video ended, and a second began. Pertinent clips from many of the original experiments came to life on the display. Tom narrated, and Catherine watched as Clyde appeared and disappeared and later as Paul and Tom, and other team members also left the current time or returned to it.

Catherine was a little less doubtful but was still apparently not entirely convinced. "So, you built a time machine that fits on a cart and named it Clyde?"

Smiling, Tom answered, "Not exactly. Equipment in our lab and the basement does most of the work. That would be what you call the time machine. Clyde is the part that makes the actual move through time.

"I know you're still doubtful, so I want to conduct a little experiment to prove to you this is real. We're going to take you back in time to make it obvious to you that this technology is real," Paul added.

Catherine promptly slid her chair back a little and felt her body become rigid. "I don't think I want to do that."

Tom started to try to discuss it further, but Paul interrupted. "Tom, there's something you're unaware of, and I don't know all the details yet, but I have a better idea."

Tom's face had a distinct look of surprise, but he didn't say anything else.

"Catherine, thirty minutes before your arrival, Tom and I set up this conference room and prepared this presentation for you. Afterward, we went to my office and shared Chinese food. When the security cameras detected your car, Tom went to let you in, and I came back to this room. Upon arriving here, I found this note and flash drive on the table. They weren't here when we left. I have read the note but have not watched the video file on the drive. You got here before I could." Paul handed Catherine the note and noticed the puzzled expression on Tom's face.

Catherine took the note and opened it. As soon as she began to read it, her face went white, and her hands shook slightly. She read it three times before setting it down.

"What's the note say?" Tom asked. The look of confusion on his face faded as his understanding began to develop.

"It appears to be a note I wrote to myself. It's clearly in my handwriting, and there's a notation at the bottom, nothing embarrassing but a trivial detail from my youth that only I would know. The problem is I never wrote this," Catherine said.

"You haven't written it yet, but you will," Paul explained.

"What's it say?" Tom asked again.

"It tells me to watch the video and believe you. It also says the video will shock me, but I should relax and believe."

Picking up the flash drive, he inserted it into the laptop connected to the LED TV. "Let's watch it then," Tom suggested.

The static appeared, and then the picture came to life. Immediately there was a gasp from Catherine as she recognized her own image on the screen. On the screen, she wore the same outfit she'd put on today and was smiling at the screen and looking a little excited.

"I know you're doubtful and a bit nervous," the voice on the screen said, "but the little demonstration they showed convinced me these guys can send someone back. I debated and resisted for two hours before reluctantly going back. So don't waste time, do it now, and you or I can get home at a decent time."

The static returned to the screen, and Tom switched off the TV.

"Wow. That was weird," she said in a low, barely audible voice.

"Let's go to the lab, and we can show you how we do this," Tom suggested.

"Well, I guess I can't argue with myself," Catherine agreed reluctantly. She stood up and followed them from the room. Heading further down the hall, they boarded an elevator that felt like it went up at least two floors. When they exited, they were in a long corridor. Several doors led off the hall, two of which went into the huge laboratory in front of the elevator.

The lab was visible through the transparent Plexiglas walls. The area was spacious and appeared neat. There were eight workstations, each with multiple computers set up at each. In the center was a large work area, and there was lots of equipment sitting there. Some of it was connected to computers and appeared as if it was still being assembled.

As they entered the lab, they headed off to the left. Catherine saw what appeared to be a modified version of the equipment cart she'd seen in the presentation. She recalled that this unit had made the first few travels through the quantum barrier. However, the cart now had four fixed seats, one on each side. The way it was configured, people would sit on the cart with their legs hanging off the sides. An encased piece of equipment was fastened to the top behind the seats. A modified laptop computer was on a flexible arm. It was positioned in front of one of the seats.

Power and data cords were running from the equipment cart to one of the walls in the lab. As they approached, Tom went to the cart and began typing on the keyboard; immediately, the equipment started humming.

"What we're going to do is take you on a brief trip back in time," Paul explained, "We won't be gone long, and we won't go back far. We need to get your complete understanding as to what we can do. Okay?"

"I guess," Catherine said hesitantly.

"The computer has already calculated the path, so come over here and take a seat opposite me," Tom said.

Paul took her arm and led her to the cart. She sat and turned her head to look over her shoulder at Tom, who was sitting opposite her, imputing commands into the computer.

"Should I put on this seat belt?" Catherine asked.

"You can if you wish. Some people feel more comfortable with it, but there's no need. You won't experience any physical movement," Tom explained.

"Will this hurt?"

"Not at all," Paul said, trying to sound reassuring, as he stood by one of the workstations in the lab.

At that moment, a voice came from somewhere on the cart. It started at six and started counting backward.

"Here we go," Tom called.

When the voice reached zero, Catherine was already holding her breath. She felt a brief shutter, and then everything seemed to go dark. Her anxiety doubled, and then Catherine realized it wasn't dark, just darker. Moments later, the lights came on.

As she started looking around, she realized Paul was gone, and Tom was walking toward her from the other side of the cart.

"You Okay?" Tom asked.

"I think so. Did we do it?"

"Sure did. I told you it would be painless," Tom said, smiling, as he took her hand and guided her off the seat.

She followed him to the door and asked, "Now what?"

"We are going to prove to you that we've gone back. We only went back a little less than an hour, but it'll make the point. Follow me."

As she followed him, she looked around, taking in a new section of the facility. Heading to the front of the building, they entered the office usually occupied by Ben Darling, Finance Officer, or so the nametag on the door said.

The room was dark, but there was enough illumination coming in from the parking lot so she could make out the contents of the room.

"Come around this way," Tom said, leading her behind the desk and to the window which overlooked the parking lot.

Looking out, she felt her heart jump when she noticed her car wasn't in the lot. For a brief moment, she feared it had been stolen, but just as quickly, she realized what was happening and what Tom wanted to show her.

After waiting several minutes, with neither saying a word, a vehicle entered the lot and approached the building. She didn't have to look at it carefully to know it was her car. She watched in amazement as it parked next to the light pole, and she saw herself get out of the car with her bag and start toward the door.

Suddenly from behind her, she heard Tom's voice call out from the hallway, "Got a good view?"

She was about to answer when she realized Tom was also beside her.

"Let's go," the Tom beside her said.

She hurried to keep up as he exited the room. Peering over the low wall, they looked down into the atrium in time to see Tom step off the escalator and head for the front door.

"This is too weird. There are two of us."

"We have to hurry now," Tom said.

Hurrying to the conference room, Tom scooped up a small video camera. "You have to make the video message so we can leave it for Paul to find."

After giving Catherine a few seconds to compose herself, he started recording. As soon as she finished, he removed the USB drive and grabbed a piece of paper.

She scooped up a pen and wrote herself a note. By this time, the questions were building in her head faster and faster, but she understood they should get out of there before anyone arrived.

They finished their work and rushed out the door. Turning the first corner, they almost ran directly into Paul, who was heading to the conference room. Everyone froze in their tracks, both sides staring at one another. Then Paul got a slight grin on his face. "Was there a problem?"

"Just a timing issue," Tom assured him. "We should arrive in just a minute."

"Good, then we should all get going. Sorry to hurry you, Professor Collins, but I need to go meet you." With a slight laugh at his own joke, Paul entered the conference room.

Tom and Catherine hurried away, and as soon as they entered the lab and the doors closed, they started laughing so hard they couldn't talk and had to sit down.

Finally, Catherine said, "I may be confused about much of this, but I know that was funny!"

"Yes, it was. We all stared at one another as if we had no idea what to do. The initial look on Paul's face was priceless."

"He did catch on quickly, though," she added.

"Once you get more familiar with how this all works, you almost find your thinking changes too. It's almost like you begin to include the concept of time travel in your day-to-day thought process."

"Well, you guys have certainly convinced me. I just don't understand what you want me for," Catherine said.

"Let's go back, and we'll go over that part," Tom suggested.

"Sounds good. Paul is sitting back there waiting for us."

"Actually, he isn't," Tom said. When he saw the puzzled look on her face, he added, "The system will return us to the exact point in time from which we left. When we get back, even though we spent over ten minutes here, we'll only have been gone a few seconds. That means if you went back in time and remained there for a full year and then returned, you would be a full year older, but only a few seconds would have gone by."

Catherine sat on the seat of the cart and began thinking about what Tom had said. As she thought about it, she realized what he meant about needing an entirely new way of thinking to follow some of these concepts. Her thoughts were interrupted by the sound of the computerized voice counting backward.

Chapter 14

Moments later, they were back in their own time. Paul was still standing where he'd been when they left. This time Catherine hopped off the seat without any hesitation or assistance.

"Okay, I'm convinced," she said.

"I know. I could see that when I saw you back there," Paul said.

Tom took only a few minutes to shut the systems down and secure the cart.

By then, Paul and Catherine had taken seats at one of the worktables.

"One thing I don't understand," Catherine said, "actually, there are several things I don't understand. I saw the recording and read the note. Those are why I was willing to go back. Once I was back there, I created the video and wrote the note I read. What if I hadn't done that when Tom and I went back? I mean, I saw and read it, but what if, when I went back, I decided that since I had already seen and read it, I wouldn't write it."

Paul nodded his understanding and answered. "That is the classic time travel paradox. You went back because of the recording, but when you went back, you decided you wouldn't bother creating it since you had seen it, so you returned. Well, now the recording would never have been made, and you would have been reluctant to go, so when you finally do go, you create the video.

"It's similar to the idea that if you go back in time and kill your mother before you were conceived, so you'll never be born and therefore won't be able to go back and kill her. So you'll be born and will then go back and kill her. There are several theories about this kind of thing. This is one of the things we're still trying to understand."

Catherine nodded her head. "That makes sense, I think. I'm going to need some quiet time to work all these new ideas out. There's still the main question. What am I here for?"

Paul smiled at her and answered. "You're here to help us settle a wager."

"What? A wager?" She asked, looking at the two men sitting across from her. There was confusion in her tone.

"Well, there's a little more to it than that," Tom explained.

"True, there is," Paul continued. "You see, now that we've proven we can do this, we've got a huge problem. What do we do with it? It's far too dangerous to allow anyone complete access to it. Let alone the fact that if word got out, there were people who could go back in time, there would be significant problems.

"Just think what would happen if everyone learned this was possible. People could provide themselves with the stock trading results for hundreds of companies. Stock trading could easily be manipulated for guaranteed gains. The stock markets of every country on the planet would completely collapse overnight and probably never recover.

"There would be the constant thought that anything which happened might have been manipulated, even if it wasn't. There would be disastrous results, possibly the complete collapse of human civilization. So, you see, we need to carefully decide who we should tell and how. One thing we'll need is a good demonstration of our abilities. Hopping in and out of time in the lab is fun and impressive, but we need something to dramatically show our capabilities. We began thinking about where to go, and I came up with the idea of a friendly wager. Tom here is very dedicated to his Christian faith. I personally don't take it seriously. I believe most religious stuff can easily be explained scientifically. Furthermore, I don't think some God is out there watching over us. Tom says there's one specific event that can prove or disprove Christianity."

"The resurrection of Christ," Catherine said.

"Exactly. We're going to go back and see it all transpire. We're going to record it and document every minute of the trip. When we return, we'll be able to not only show our abilities but offer proof to the world. Proof to answer one of the greatest debates of all time."

"Ok, I see that, but where does the wager come in?"

Before Paul could respond, Tom answered. "If the resurrection didn't occur, then Christ was just a teacher. An excellent and effective teacher, but just a man and not God. I don't believe for a second, we'll come to that conclusion. But for the sake of argument, if we do, there have been billions of Christians over time wasting their time and resources for nothing. I would be obligated under the terms of the wager to let the world know."

Paul continued. "Also, if there's a God, and we prove the resurrection did occur, then I don't want to be on his bad side. If there are things he directs me and others to do, I want to be right on board with him. Suppose there truly was a resurrection as my part of the wager, I'll commit myself to using the information we bring back to prove to as many people as possible that we must follow Christ."

"That is a mighty big wager; one of you'll be experiencing some major changes in your life," Catherine commented.

Paul nodded and added, "The way I see it, there's a huge question out there. Once we find the answer, we'll share what we've learned. Neither of us is saying we'll shave our heads and sit on a street corner shouting for people to believe or not believe. But, we'll do what we can to tell people what we've learned."

"And what is my part in this expedition to be?" Catherine asked.

"We need background information about the time period and the culture. We'll also need some rudimentary language skills. We need to be able to blend in with the crowds. We're going to record the events as they transpire, but we need to make sure we don't stand out," Tom explained.

"We'll keep to ourselves and avoid situations that require more than minimal social interaction. Our clothes, actions, and even mannerisms must be authentic. We'll need to ensure we're carrying the appropriate items that people from that time would've had," Paul added.

"I think you two are insane," Catherine said. "You honestly think you can drop into a strange culture whose languages you don't speak and successfully wander around for a day and record a specific event without detection? What if you're approached or confronted? Also, do you really think I can give you the language skills needed to keep anyone from becoming suspicious? How many years do you plan to prepare for this journey? Because it'll take years to get you two ready for something like this."

"Actually, Professor," Paul said, "we plan to be there for more than just one day." He knew this didn't help his argument, but it was all he had at the moment.

"How long are you planning on staying?"

"That's still to be determined. Our people are still working on the technology; it'll depend on the systems' power consumption. You see, once you get there, all the data for the return trip resides on the onboard computers that go with you.

If they lose power, all the data for the return is gone, and coming back is impossible. So power consumption and battery life are huge issues," Paul explained.

"Why can't the return data be saved to a hard drive and retrieved when the system restarts? You could then remain indefinitely as long as you could bring the system back up," she asked.

"It isn't just a map home that's on the systems. There's an active link we must maintain. Think of it like this. If you call someone's cell phone and they answer, you can keep the connection established even if no one speaks. But if the cell phone's battery dies, you're through. In our situation, we can't initiate the call between systems that are in different times; we can maintain it but not initiate it."

Catherine's interest was peaked, and it showed in all the questions she asked. "You said the actual time machine is here in the basement. How will you transport something so massive halfway around the world so you can go back to Israel?"

"Great question," Tom said, glad she appeared interested. "We couldn't transport it, even if we had to. It's too big.

"The relationship between time and space is extremely complex. To go back in time, there's a folding of both space and time. We can appear at any time and any place. If you sign on, you'll eventually understand the basics of how it works."

"Does that mean you can teleport?"

Paul answered, "In a sense, we are teleporting to a different time and, in some cases, a different location. Without the folding of time, we cannot change location. So we cannot change locations without changing times."

"However, that's one of the next areas we'll be taking this project. Teleporting within the same timeline should be possible. Since we've gotten this far, that's the next logical step. We just haven't had the time or resources to chase that down yet," Tom added.

Catherine nodded and then continued, "So, how long are you hoping to stay in the past?"

"Four days minimum. We want to record the Crucifixion, but if we can get there a few days before that, it would be good," Tom answered. "But as things stand now, we'd need to each carry over one hundred pounds of batteries. We couldn't show up on a utility cart. That would be much too conspicuous; we need to have everything mobile. We're working on backpack versions of the equipment, but it'll be a few months before we can test it. After that, we'll focus on reducing power consumption."

"When do you hope to make the trip back?" Catherine asked.

"That depends on two things. How long it takes to get the new backpacks ready and for you to prepare us. We have other consultants who will be involved too."

"You do?" Catherine asked. There was an apparent annoyance in her voice.

"No, Catherine. It isn't anything like that," Tom said with a smile. "We don't know what situations we might get into, and we want to prepare for any problems. If we run into trouble, we need to be able to defend ourselves without doing anyone any actual harm.

"If we took a firearm back for protection and killed someone, the chances their death would considerably change the future are enormous. Consider that not only are we taking his life, but the life of every one of their decedents. It could literally be tens of thousands of people. Then you factor in the impact these people had on others. Those interactions would now never happen, and millions of people would be affected. The chances are low none of those people had some vital role in their time. We must ensure our presence there doesn't result in someone's death. Also, it isn't only that we must make sure we don't kill anyone, but saving someone who would have otherwise died could be just as disastrous for the opposite reason.

"So we've got a consultant coming who will teach us techniques to defend ourselves, a condensed martial arts class for lack of a better description. We'll also train with other non-lethal devices. There'll also be some first aid training in case we get into trouble and don't want to abort and come back.

"There will be some specialized equipment we aren't familiar with that we'll be using, and there'll be training in that too. We're still assembling a list of all the other things we need to know and be ready for, just in case something unexpected comes up."

"It sounds like you're working through most of this, but my original objection is still the same; you won't have adequate language skills to remain undetected in that culture, especially if you try to remain there for several days. I can help you prepare, but your chances of succeeding remain remote. However, there's a way we could greatly increase your chances of success," Catherine said.

"What are you thinking?" Paul asked hesitantly.

"I need to go with you," Catherine stated.

"What! Are you kidding?" Paul exclaimed.

"I don't think so," Tom said simultaneously.

"Well, why not? I'm an expert in the time period. I understand the culture. I know both the Latin and Aramaic languages. I'm familiar with the geography and can even draw rudimentary maps of Jerusalem from memory. If you're to succeed, I'll be invaluable." Catherine explained.

"All that's true," Tom admitted, "That just isn't what we envisioned for this trip."

Paul looked at them silently, and after a few moments, he nodded and said, "We will need to think about it."

"Ok, I can understand that. But when you discuss it, try to come up with a few reasons why my going would be a problem and compare it with what I've got to offer."

"We will," Tom assured her. "If we decide against it, are you still interested in helping us prepare for the trip?"

"Certainly, I wouldn't miss it."

"Good. Any suggestions of where we should start?" Paul asked.

"Sure, there are two things. First, join a gym and work out as much as possible. You'll be doing lots of walking and carrying some heavy equipment," Catherine explained.

Paul nodded. "That is in the plan already."

"Good. Also, don't either of you get a haircut. Short hair wasn't normal, and unless you want to spend several days in an uncomfortable wig, you'll let it grow out as much as possible. Also, stop shaving. A beard is needed if you don't want to stand out."

"See, she's proving valuable already," Tom said, looking at Paul.

"One thing just came to mind," Paul said. "We need to know the exact date we wish to travel back to. Is the actual date of the crucifixion known?"

"Historians have studied this for years. There are records from that time, as well as Biblical references. From all the information, the most widely agreed date is Friday, April 3, A.D. 33. There are those who disagree and say it's A.D. 30, but the numbers don't all fit as well for that to work.

I would suggest starting from there. If it turns out you're too late, we will learn what we can and pick the other date," Catherine explained.

Smiling, Paul said. "More great information! It's getting late, and we all have a lot to consider. We'll discuss you going with us. Could you start planning lessons to help us learn about the times? And call or stop by in a few days, and we'll set a training schedule. If you want, we can set you up in an office here. I don't know if that'll help."

"Sounds like a good start. It'll make it easier for me if you have an office available." Catherine agreed.

When they'd finished the discussion, Tom led Catherine to the front door. "Next time you're here, we'll have an ID badge waiting for you."

"Good, that will make things easier."

After continuing the conversation for a little longer, Tom and Paul walked their new teacher to the door.

Chapter 15

LATE THE NEXT AFTERNOON, TOM KNOCKED ON PAUL'S OFFICE door, stepped in, and took a seat when he saw his friend wasn't busy.

"Sorry, I didn't get in to discuss what happened last night with you earlier. Steph got her braces today, and I took the morning to be with her at the orthodontist's office," Tom explained.

"I remember you mentioning it. How did it go?"

"She was nervous but didn't complain. I think she'll be a little sore but will adjust."

"Good. I'm glad you went. That's where you needed to be," Paul stated.

"Are you guys still coming to dinner tonight?" Tom inquired.

"Absolutely. I'll be done here in a few minutes, then I'm going home to get Michelle, and we'll be there by six."

"Good. Linda and the kids are looking forward to seeing you guys."

After briefly pausing the conversation, Tom asked, "Well, what did you think of Catherine?"

Paul looked up from his computer screen and nodded

briefly, "She seems quite knowledgeable about the time period, and she's very interested in the project."

"I agree," Tom said, "How do you feel about her going with us?"

"I don't know. Part of me wants to say no, this is our thing. You know what I mean?"

Tom nodded, "That's how I initially felt when she suggested it."

Then Paul continued, "But she makes sense. We don't know the area or the culture. For that point, we can't even speak the language. I guess I'm not ready to admit we need an outsider to hold our hands through this."

"Think of it this way. We'll need a minimum of six months to prepare for this. By then, she won't be an outsider anymore."

"True," Paul agreed.

"So, are you going to call her, or do you want me to?" Tom inquired.

"I'll do it, but not until at least tomorrow. I don't want to seem too anxious to have her come along."

Tom laughed and headed out of the office.

Paul returned to his computer and finished the document he was reading on the screen. Fifteen minutes later, he logged off the computer and, picking up his bag, headed out the door. A reminder alarm sounded on his phone as he walked toward his car. Glancing at it, he saw the message read, "Meat."

Typically when he and Michelle went to someone's house for dinner, they'd bring a nice bottle of wine. In this case, he knew Tom and Linda didn't drink often. Neither he nor Michelle cooked and certainly couldn't make anything well enough to impress someone else. So Paul had offered to bring the steaks. Tom had said it wasn't necessary, but Paul had insisted.

Michelle was supposed to have called the butcher shop to

have them ready when he arrived. He hoped she remembered because he didn't feel like standing around waiting for the butcher to cut them.

Parking as close to the store as possible, Paul enjoyed the sun's warmth as he walked inside.

Since he was a little short on time and didn't want to show up late, he hoped he wouldn't run into anyone he knew and have to spend time talking. He was usually sociable but preferred to keep moving when he had somewhere to be. Fortunately, within five minutes of pulling into the parking lot, he was leaving with two hundred and seventeen dollars' worth of hand-trimmed rib eye steaks.

As he drove, Paul told the vehicle to text Michelle and let her know his progress. When he pulled up to the house, Michelle promptly came out and climbed in.

As they drove along, they discussed the wager. "Is Tom as excited about this as you are?" Michelle asked.

"Maybe even more so, but for different reasons. The real purpose of this whole thing is to prove our process works and have a dramatic way of showing the world what we can do. That's what I'm excited about.

"Tom feels the same way. However, the wager has him all fired up in a new way too. To him, he's going to get to see Jesus, and that means everything. We might even find a way to speak to him. I'm not as interested in the outcome of the wager. I just want to have proof, either way, which we can use to generate excitement for our work at the institute," Paul explained.

"I know it isn't something we discuss much, but do you think you'll win?" She asked.

"I have a problem with the idea of an all-powerful God. Too much here is screwed up for there to be someone who could fix it all with the snap of his fingers."

"I understand what you're saying, but I grew up in the church. I may not be there at this point in my life, but I remember what I learned, and I can't write it off. I wish you luck, but I'm not sure you'll win this."

Paul laughed and said, "Thanks for the support."

As they pulled into Tom's driveway, Michelle replied, "Sorry, nothing personal." She hoped she hadn't made him mad but wasn't too concerned. In the year and a half they'd known each other, she'd seen about every possible human emotion from Paul except anger. He once told her that he seldom becomes angry, but it can be ugly when he does.

Exiting the vehicle, the couple headed to the house. Before they could knock, the door opened, and the two youngest Wallace children, Matthew and Mallory, came out to greet them. "Hi Paul, Hi Michelle," the kids said in unison.

"Hey, guys," Paul greeted them.

"Where is Stephanie?" Michelle asked.

"She's in watching TV. She got her braces today and isn't doing anything but lying around," the seven-year-old Mallory answered.

"Ouch, that's no fun," Michelle stated. "When I was a kid, I had to wear braces for three years. Maybe I'll go talk to her."

While Michelle went in search of the eldest Wallace child, the others led Paul to the back patio, where Tom and Linda were sitting.

"I brought meat!" Paul declared, holding up the package wrapped in butcher's paper.

"Great. I'll get the grill going," Tom said.

"That looks like enough to feed the whole neighborhood," Linda said as she gave Paul a friendly hug.

"I wasn't sure how much to get, so I got seven."

"These are monsters," Tom stated as he unwrapped the steaks. "No one will go hungry tonight."

Looking around, Linda asked, "Where'd Michelle go?"

"She has many years of personal experience with braces. She went to talk to Steph," Paul explained.

"Good. Steph handled it well but has been a bit down since we got home."

"Maybe I'll have to eat some thick steak in front of her," Paul joked.

Linda laughed and punched him in the arm.

When the rib eyes were perfectly grilled, and the rest of the food had come out of the house, the seven of them sat down to eat.

Paul and Michelle waited respectfully while Tom said a prayer of thanks for the food.

Michelle showed Stephanie she could eat some if she cut the meat small enough.

As the meal progressed, Michelle asked, "So Linda, what do you think of this wager?"

"I think it sounds exciting. I'm most concerned about what dangers there might be in the past that these guys would have to deal with. No offense to our men, but today's men aren't exactly as tough as those of biblical times."

Michelle added, "At least they smartened up enough to agree to bring a woman along to keep them out of trouble."

As both women laughed at this, all Paul and Tom did was glance at each other and say nothing.

"Will you guys really get to meet Jesus? My dad says you might," Matthew asked Paul.

"I don't know Matt. We plan to see him at least."

"That is so cool!" the Wallace boy replied.

Paul regarded his friend. "You're rather quiet about this. Are you having second thoughts? Think you might lose?" He teased.

"I'm struggling," Tom admitted, "but not about winning. I'm not concerned about that because I truly believe. What I'm struggling with is the concept of faith. Faith is a key ingredient in Christianity. Romans 5:1 says that we're saved by faith in Christ. The importance of faith is mentioned over and over in the Bible. Faith means that we believe without proof.

Suppose we obtain proof and show it to the world. In that case, many more will believe. But it won't be because of faith, but because of our evidence," Tom paused, then continued, "I'm concerned about the implications of that."

Everyone got quiet for a little while, and then Linda spoke. "Do you not want to go? Maybe go to a different time period and event?"

After a quiet pause, Tom answered, "No, we're going. I just need to think and pray through these thoughts."

The rest of the evening's conversation was much lighter. Both women wanted to talk to Catherine about the adventure. By the time Paul and Michelle headed home, it was quite late.

Chapter 16

OVER THE NEXT SEVERAL MONTHS, TOM AND PAUL LEARNED more about the ancient Middle East than they'd ever expected to know. They developed the ability to understand conversational Aramaic, Latin, and even a little Hebrew. However, they spent very little time speaking. Their limited speaking wasn't much more than single-word answers to common questions.

The men and Catherine spent many hours learning general hand-to-hand combat skills. While their abilities were increasing, the progress was slow since Paul insisted they do all training with a seventy-pound pack on their backs.

The three of them had taken to wearing the packs at all times when there were at the Kingsman Research Institute. At first, the load had felt unbearable, but over time they'd adapted, and their stamina increased.

Other areas of their training included some general first aid, survival, and camouflage and concealment. Because there was always the possibility they'd have to hide for a while if they began to draw suspicion.

Catherine joined Tom and Paul in the training room one afternoon for a 2 pm training session. She was surprised to see an unfamiliar man at the front of the room.

Seeing her enter, Paul said, "Catherine, this is Raymond Chandler. He'll be showing us some interesting tools we hopefully won't ever need."

Raymond walked to Catherine and held out his hand, which she shook.

"Hi, Catherine. Please call me Ray."

Smiling, Catherine said, "Hi, what will we be learning today?"

Paul explained, "We might need to defend ourselves, and Ray has a couple of non-lethal devices which could help us."

Catherine glanced at the table and saw a couple of odd looking items.

The first item was shaped similarly to a handgun but, upon closer evaluation, was much different. The second was a black canister. It stood about four inches high and had a trigger on the top.

As the trio gathered around the table, Ray picked up the item Tom thought resembled a toy plastic gun.

Ray said, "This is the M26 Taser pistol. Instead of firing a potentially lethal bullet, this weapon, when fired, shoots out two small darts attached to wires which run back to the gun. Upon contact with the target, fifty thousand volts travels down the wires and enters the person, instantly disrupting the body's central nervous system. Pass it around; this is a training taser; it can't hurt you."

After examining the Taser pistol, Paul asked, "What if the target has clothing where the darts hit?"

"Good question; the darts will penetrate several layers of clothing," Ray explained.

Catherine asked, "How long are the wires? What is the range?"

"The wires are fifteen feet long, so the target needs to be somewhere closer than that for it to work."

"Fifty thousand volts sounds like a lot. How much damage will this do to someone?" Tom wanted to know.

Nodding, Ray said, "Fifty thousand sounds like a lot, but there's no permanent effect because of the low amperage. However, the target will be disabled for several minutes. I have a video we'll watch to show all this in detail."

"What about this one?" Catherine asked, holding up the black cylinder.

"That's OC pepper spray. What comes out is derived from hot pepper plants. One spray in the face of an attacker, and they wouldn't be a threat for at least several minutes. One thing to be careful when using this is to ensure you aren't spraying into any wind or breeze, or you will get yourself as well as the target, and it isn't a pleasant experience."

Sitting down, the trio watched the video, which showed both devices in use. They were impressed with what they saw on the Tazer demo. The subject, when shot, instantly dropped to the ground, and all their muscles contracted, leaving them in a fetal position. The target was able to get up within a couple of minutes, but it was several additional minutes before they'd be any threat.

When the video was over, and they'd practiced with both devices, the trio thanked Ray, and Tom walked him out.

While Tom was gone, Paul asked, "Do you have any concerns with either of those devices?"

Shaking her head, Catherine said, "No. I hope we don't need them, but I'll feel more comfortable knowing we have them.

ALL THREE OF them enjoyed the medical, hand-to-hand combat, and non-lethal weapon training. However, they spent most of their efforts on language skills and enhancing their understanding of the culture.

After several months of working on the languages, they were eventually able to engage one another in simple conversations. Soon they began incorporating the languages into their daily routine. Paul and Tom communicated in Aramaic or Latin when possible. Catherine often refused to speak English to them unless they were in the middle of a lesson she was giving. Their vocabulary was extremely limited, and they didn't understand the written languages.

As time progressed, their co-workers became more and more amused with the company's leaders. They were always walking around with backpacks on, speaking in strange tongues. Their unusual appearance, with lengthening hair and beards, only added to the amusement. They both appeared less and less professional all the time.

One of the most challenging parts of their preparation was outfitting themselves to fit in with the general population. They'd all wear loose-fitting cloaks to hide the outlines of the backpacks. Their garments would have concealed pockets for holding tools, cameras, food, medical supplies, and weapons. They would each wear a waist pouch containing batteries and additional high-capacity storage drives for the video cameras.

Most of the cameras were extremely high-tech and attached under their garments. They would film through small holes no larger than a pencil eraser.

Catherine spent many hours studying texts and even traveling to museums to better research the clothing designs and the types of objects people from that time period carried.

The more she learned, the more concerned she became regarding their ability to keep from being noticed in that strange time period. There were very few artifacts from that period to give much information as to how garments were assembled. Let alone the types of items individuals routinely carried. Somehow they needed better information before plunging themselves into a different time and trying to blend in.

Chapter 17

THE 64-YEAR-OLD WOMAN SLEPT PEACEFULLY IN THE QUEEN-sized bed that she shared with no one. She lived alone and had done so since her husband passed away years before.

The alarm in her phone sounded, ripping her from her peaceful slumber. Reaching over, she silenced it, then lay back down and closed her eyes for another minute. Then she threw off the covers and sat on the side of the bed and, as she had begun doing recently, wondered why she was still getting up like this each day.

She had enough money in the bank, and her retirement accounts were healthy enough to retire now, and she knew it would be time soon. But currently, she still enjoyed her job and the people she worked with.

After taking a few deep breaths, she stretched her arms and back, working out the stiffness which had settled into her aging body during the night.

Eventually, the widow rose, put on her robe, and headed to the kitchen. Taking a tea bag from the jar on the counter, she dropped it in a mug and filled it with water before sticking it in the microwave.

She headed to the shower as the water heated and the tea leaves steeped.

Five minutes later, as she dressed, the woman glanced out the window and saw a lot of fresh snow and ice. Again she wondered why she was still going to work and considered calling in sick. It was something she often considered but never did. She had a commitment to her employer, and as long as she worked there, she would honor it.

Once dressed, she took the tea from the microwave and, leaving the bag behind, poured the hot liquid into her travel cup.

After getting on her white winter coat and boots, she picked up the cup of tea and the zipped bag containing her work shoes and headed for the door. Glancing at the clock, she saw that she needed to hurry. The bus to take her into the city would be coming soon.

There was snow and ice everywhere, and she considered calling her son to have him come and clear the steps for her, but she knew it was unnecessary. He'd be by at some point today; he always was. She was thankful he was so dependable.

She stepped into the ice-covered spot on the top step, turned, and used her key to secure the deadbolt.

Turning back, she carefully stepped down the first of the three steps, unable to hold the rail because her hands were occupied with the bag and cup of tea.

Continuing to descend, she stepped off the bottom step and onto the icy walkway. That's when her boots suddenly flew out from under her.

The fall was fast and hard. As she went down, the back of her head struck the edge of the second step with significant force, and she was unconscious instantly.

A car was going by as she descended the stairs and had past by right before the fall happened. The driver missed the event by only a second or two.

Now flat on her back and unconscious, wearing an all-white coat that blended in with the snow, it would be several hours before the mail carrier on his regular route would discover the nearly frozen woman.

Chapter 18

TOM SAT ACROSS FROM PAUL AT A LOCAL STEAKHOUSE. THE two of them didn't often go out to lunch together. Both usually preferred to bring their food with them and continue working through lunch. However, Paul had suggested taking this break, saying they needed to celebrate all the progress they'd been having, and Tom had agreed.

Catherine was teaching at the university today, so they'd considered rescheduling for a day when she could join them, but she'd insisted they go. She'd said that she was still a newcomer to the team and the two old friends should enjoy some time together.

It was nice to relax occasionally, and they both knew they'd not done this enough. It seemed the more success they had, the more they wanted to work hard to accomplish more.

They had come close to canceling these lunch plans today. There had been a big storm early this morning, and six inches of icy, wet snow was on the ground. The storm had started with freezing rain, which put a treacherous layer of ice under the snow. They'd both seen several accidents on their way to work and weren't sure if they wanted to go out. Fortunately, the roads had improved since their initial travel this morning, and they got to the restaurant without incident.

Paul had tried to steer the conversation away from work initially, but that only lasted until they placed their orders, then the discussion slid back to business.

"This training is much more time consuming than I expected," Paul stated.

"I know, I want to work on some of the technical details, but I'm always in class preparing for the trip," Tom acknowledged. "It's good that our team is so competent; they're getting much of the system redesign done with little input from us."

As Paul was about to respond, their food arrived. Each had ordered a small steak. Paul had steak fries with his, and Tom got the seasoned rice.

"Does everything look right?" the waiter said.

The men cut into their steaks, and Tom sighed and almost said something when he saw the inside of the steak had no pink to it. He'd explicitly asked for it medium rare. Thinking about how long it would take to recook the meat, he decided to accept it as is.

"It's okay," he answered, and the waiter left.

Their conversation died off as they ate.

About halfway through the meal, Tom's cell phone rang. Glancing at the screen, he saw it was a local number that was unfamiliar. He paused briefly, considering letting the voicemail pick it up, but at the last minute chose to answer.

Paul glanced up when the phone rang and saw the quizzical look on his friend's face. He tried not to pay too close attention to Tom's call, but being directly across from him made it impossible.

"Hello?" After a brief pause, Paul heard, "Yes, this is Tom Wallace."

Following a slightly longer delay, he saw the color drain from Tom's face. "Yes, I am. What happened?"

Tom's speech was now noticeably faster. "Is she okay?"

"How bad?"

"What else can you tell me?"

"Ok, I'm on my way." As he said this, he pressed the button to end the call."

Even before the call ended, Paul signaled the waiter for the check. He looked at his friend, the distress evident on his face. "What happened?"

"It's my mom. She is in the hospital. She didn't show up for work, and they couldn't reach her by phone, so they sent someone to her house and the ambulance was already there. Sounds like she slipped on the icy steps and hit her head." After a pause, he continued. "I was going to stop there on my way home and clean up all the ice and snow."

The waiter arrived with their check, "Do you want any boxes?" He asked.

Paul handed him his credit card and said, "No, but we're in a hurry and need to go."

Sensing the mood change at the table, he gave Paul a quick nod and disappeared with the card.

As they waited, Paul asked, "Did they tell you any more?"

"Just that they think she was laying out in the snow for several hours, and there's bleeding in her brain."

When he heard this, Paul said. "I'll take you directly to the hospital as soon as we get out of here. You should call Linda and let her know."

Tom nodded, slipped on his coat, and headed for the door with his phone in his hand already dialing.

While Paul waited for the waiter's return, he went back to his meal while thinking of his friend. He'd met Deb Wallace a few times and thought of her as a lovely person. Her husband, Tom's father, had died of heart disease about ten years ago. Shortly after Tom started at the Kingsman Research Institute, she'd relocated here from California to be near Tom and his family.

She was young enough that she didn't need Tom checking in on her, though she was considering retirement in the next few years. Each day she commuted to work in the city on the bus, and Tom said she was growing tired of it.

Deb was in charge of advertising for a group of radio stations. It was an excellent job for her, which she'd quickly got upon moving to the area. Deb had extensive advertising experience, which she brought when taking the job. Tom had been pleased when she'd recently mentioned that she was considering retiring. She wanted to travel while she was still young enough.

The waiter approached with the credit card and receipt and noticed Paul still picking at his food.

"Sir, are you sure you don't want a box?"

"No, it's okay. I need to get my friend to the hospital." Paul replied, not thinking about what the waiter might think of that statement. Before the man could respond, Paul was up, took the card, and headed for the door.

As he exited, he saw his friend pacing back and forth next to the car with his phone to his ear.

When Tom noticed Paul, he ended the call and climbed into the passenger side. Paul got in and headed for the highway.

"Is Linda going to meet us there?" Paul asked his distressed friend.

"Yes. She's finishing something up and will be there as soon as possible."

Paul tried several times to engage his friend in conversation, but it became clear he didn't want to talk. At one point, Paul thought he heard Tom say something, glanced over, and realized the grieving man was praying.

They made good time, with the SUV zipping in and out of traffic. While the driving would seem quite aggressive to some, it wasn't much more so than Paul's normal behavior behind the wheel. Tom didn't react to the extreme driving; his mind was on his mother.

Tom had considered stopping at her house before work but instead decided to make sure she was dug out on his way home tonight. He wasn't sure how severe her injuries were, but his feelings of guilt were already very heavy.

Arriving at the emergency entrance, Paul slowed to a stop. "I'll park and meet you inside," he said.

"You don't have to stay; Linda will be here soon."

Paul replied, "I am staying until she gets here."

Tom shut the door and headed for the entrance. As he walked in, he glanced around the waiting room at the unhappy people waiting their turn for care. A little less than half the seats were occupied. This gave Tom hope the ER wasn't busy and his mother's care was moving quickly.

Approaching the desk, Tom waited while the woman working there finished up with a man who was holding a young child with a bloody bandage on his forearm. When they stepped aside, he moved up. "My mother, Debra Wallace, was brought in by ambulance."

The woman nodded, picked up the phone, and spoke, "I have the son of Debra Wallace here. Can he come back?" After a few seconds, she hung it up.

"Please step over to those doors. Someone is on the way to get you." As she spoke, she pointed to a set of blue steel, windowless doors adjacent to the registration desks.

Tom walked toward them, and as he approached, they swung open, revealing a tall young woman in blue scrubs who made eye contact with Tom.

"Mr. Wallace?"

Tom nodded, "Yes."

"Please come with me; I'll take you to your mother."

As they walked along, Tom was aware of the smell of disinfectant and other things he couldn't place. The woman led him past treatment rooms, and he saw patients in gowns and staff in scrubs. Someone was moaning in a room they passed where the curtain blocked the view of what was taking place. Most of the treatment areas were small and only had curtains to separate the patients.

After making a turn, a set of glass doors slid apart as they passed through. Inside were about a dozen treatment areas, all much larger and with much more complicated equipment. Only four were occupied, and they headed to a room near the middle. Tom could see a patient in the bed but not their face, and he assumed it was his mom.

His eyes were taking in all he was seeing. Several IV bags were hanging by the head of the bed. Wires were coming out from under the blankets and attached to a machine with an EKG display. There were many other devices and screens with information displayed. Tom was more focused on the tube coming up from her mouth. It was connected to flexible hoses attached to a machine beside the bed. Even before Tom was to the bed, he could hear the rhythmic way it pushed oxygen into his mother's lungs every few seconds.

Slowly approaching, he got right next to the bed. He stared down at her face and could recognize his mom, even with the tube secured in her mouth with a strap around her head. There was also a bandage on the back of the head, and the wrapping obscured the forehead. There was an odd device attached to the top of her head. It looked to Tom like a dart stuck deep in the skull. Coming off of it was a wire which plugged into another monitor. She didn't appear to be awake.

"Mr. Wallace?" said a voice from behind him.

Tom turned and saw a man in maroon scrubs. He was medium height and had a mustache. "Yes."

"I'm Mike; I'm your mother's nurse. We spoke on the phone," He explained.

"I'm Tom. How's she doing?"

"Not good, I'm afraid. When your mother fell, she hit her head on the concrete step. The CAT scan shows there's heavy bleeding in her brain." He paused briefly to let Tom absorb the information before continuing. "EMS was called at 10:30. Do you know where she was going and at what time?" The nurse asked.

"She leaves the house at 7 am to go to work."

"Well, that means she laid out in the snow and ice for nearly three and a half hours. When she came in, she was quite hypothermic. The hypothermia might have saved her. Everything slows down when the body temperature drops. We have warming blankets on her, and we're giving her heated IV fluids. Her core temperature is much better. The neurosurgeon was in here a little while ago. He needs to get the artery in her head fixed. She has too much pressure on her brain from all the bleeding and swelling there."

Tom asked, "When will they do the surgery?"

"They are getting the OR ready now, and should be down to get her in the next ten minutes or so," Mike explained.

"Has she been awake at all since she got here?"

"No. When the paramedics arrived at her house, she was unresponsive, and that hasn't changed."

"What's that thing in the top of her head?"

"It's monitoring the pressure in her brain. It's critical the pressure doesn't get too high, so we're closely watching it.

Tom carefully asked the following question, afraid of what the answer would be. "Will she wake up after the surgery?"

Mike had suspected this question was coming. He hated to hear it because there was no right way to answer it. "It'll depend on how much damage there is. These things aren't possible to accurately predict. After the surgeon gets a look inside, he might have a better idea. But even then, we'll have to wait and see if and when she wakes up."

Tom wasn't surprised by the answer. It wasn't what he'd wanted to hear, but it was what he suspected Mike would say. Reaching down, he took his mother's hand and was shocked at how cold it was. Her body temperature hadn't returned to normal yet. He closed his eyes to pray when suddenly something was making a loud alarm sound. Looking up, he didn't notice any change in her appearance, but the machine with the wire which went into her head flashed several numbers and bright red lights.

Several people rushed into the room and asked Tom to leave. Stepping outside the curtain, he listened as they fought to stabilize his mother. He could see a little around the edge of the curtain and saw Nurse Mike pick up a telephone handset on the wall.

"Shelly, this is Mike in the ED. Are you ready for Mrs. Wallace?" after a pause, he continued. "Her ICP spiked, and we need to get her up there now." Another long pause, and then he finished. "Good. No, we'll bring her up now."

There was more muted conversation, and then another voice said, "Let's get her moving."

The curtain slid open, and Tom moved out of the way as his mom's hospital bed advanced, along with most of the equipment connected to her. They were in a big hurray, and the bed moved away rapidly.

Tom felt numb and lost as to what to do when he felt people close behind him. Turning, he saw Paul and Linda standing there, also looking lost.

Linda grabbed his upper arm and pulled him close. "Paul told me what happened; I'm so sorry."

Tom nodded, "They rushed out so fast. That has to be a bad sign."

The tall woman in blue scrubs returned. This time Tom noticed her nametag read Andrea and that she was a student nurse. "Mr. Wallace, I can take you to the Neuro-Surgical waiting room."

Linda replied, "You don't have to take us. Can you just give directions?"

Smiling, she answered, "This is an old building with many additions over the years. It's a bit of a complicated route."

"Thank you, sorry to tie you up like this," Linda replied.

As they started to walk, Tom turned to his friend, "Paul, we're okay. There's no need for you to stay. She'll probably be in surgery for several hours. I really appreciate your getting me here and staying until Linda arrived."

"Are you sure? I don't mind," Paul responded.

"Yeah, I'm sure. I promise to call when we know something."

"You better call, no matter what time it is. Do you need any help with the kids?

Linda answered, "No. They're staying with our neighbor. They hang out over there with their kids all the time, so it isn't a problem. But, thanks."

Paul put his hand on his friend's shoulder and said, "I'm sorry about all this. Let me know if there's anything I can do."

Chapter 19

TOM AND LINDA FOLLOWED ANDREA TO THE NEURO-SURGICAL waiting area and checked in with the female attendant. Tom provided their contact information, and she assured them that if she got any information, she'd pass it along. Otherwise, the surgical resident would meet with them after the surgery. They estimated they'd finish in the operating room in about four hours, but the timing could change as things developed.

The attendant provided directions to the cafeteria and informed them that if they were planning to go, they should do it sooner rather than closer to the expected time the surgery would be completed. Thanking the woman for the help, they chose seats near the back of the room and in the corner where they'd hopefully be alone because they weren't in a sociable mood. They sat and prayed together for a few minutes and then sat and waited.

After about thirty minutes, Linda excused herself and went downstairs to the cafeteria. Neither of them was hungry, but Tom's lunch had been interrupted, and she'd missed her's entirely. Linda moved through the line looking for items she could take back to the waiting room, which would still be good if they didn't get eaten immediately.

.She passed by some pizza that looked like it had come out of a box many hours earlier. The burgers looked a little better, but the fries which went with them were pale and limp. She settled on the make-it-yourself sandwich bar. She took some rye bread, made a couple of roast beef sandwiches with everything they liked, and returned to the room.

On the way back, she was a little conflicted. She wanted to be there for Tom when the surgeon returned but also hoped she'd missed him and the waiting would be over. She walked in and saw Tom was still alone. She sat next to him, and together they picked at the food and waited for another three hours before someone walked up to them.

"Mr. and Mrs. Wallace, I'm Doctor Mounard. I'm the surgical resident assigned to your mother's case."

Tom tried to sound friendly and smiled but replied, "How's she doing? How'd it go?"

"May I sit for a minute?" the doctor asked.

Linda replied, "Of course, please do."

Moving a chair so it sat across from them, he sat and spoke, "The surgery went well. We were able to repair the damaged artery and evacuate most of the blood. However, the leaked blood and swelling caused significant pressure on your mother's brain. All that pressure can collapse blood vessels that weren't injured and may affect blood flow to areas of the brain where there wasn't any trauma. Right now, that's our biggest concern. The big question is how much of her brain was affected by the pressure that the injury caused. Does this make sense?"

Nodding, Tom replied, "I think so."

"Okay. She's in the recovery area now and will be for another twenty minutes or so. We'll then take her for another CT scan and an additional test. Afterward, she'll be in the Nero ICU. That's two floors up from here. I expect you'll be able to see her in about an hour and a half. I'll get you pointed in the direction of the ICU waiting room, but first, are there any questions I can answer for you?"

"I assume you can't give us any prognosis until you get the results of these next two tests?" Tom asked.

"That is correct. There's nothing I can say now with any degree of certainty."

"Ok. Thank you for all you have done." Tom said.

"Of course. I hope we'll have more information in a few hours. Dr. Koptin, the attending neurosurgeon, or I'll be up in the ICU when they let you back."

They both verified their understanding to the young doctor. Standing, he added, "If you want to follow me, I'll show you where the waiting room of the Neuro ICU is. I'm already going that way," he said. As they left, the woman at the reception desk crossed their names off the list of patients waiting to hear the results of their loved one's surgeries.

Chapter 20

TOM AND LINDA SAT WAITING AGAIN WHILE SIPPING FROM coffee cups. The complimentary beverages and snacks in the ICU waiting area were nice. Still, they both desperately wanted to get out of the room. All of the hours of waiting had been quite tiring. Neither wanted to miss being called back, so they sat and endured the monotonous wait. Both had texted or called family and friends to let them know what had developed.

The TV in the corner was on, and Tom had tried to distract himself by focusing on the shows, but it hadn't worked. Each time he quickly was gone into his dark thoughts again.

Finally, the door opened, and Tom heard his name called. Together they stood and approached the door. There was a nurse in maroon scrubs there to greet them. "My name is Toni, and I'll be your mother's nurse for the next hour. My replacement will introduce herself when she arrives."

Tom and Linda shared their names with Toni and followed her into the Neurological Intensive Care Unit. Again, the area had a disinfectant smell. There were about twelve patient rooms. Unlike in the Emergency Department, all the patient rooms were separated by transparent glass walls instead of curtains.

They headed to the right and were moving toward one of the last rooms when several people nearly pushed them out of the way running in the same direction. Tom could see the sign outside the second to last room with his mother's name on it. His skin grew cold as the doctors and nurses ran in that direction. He was briefly relieved when they entered the room beside his mother's and raced to save its occupant. Now since he knew his mother wasn't the one needing all the extra attention, his concern went to the person who was her neighbor.

That concern was short-lived. As soon as he passed through the doors into his mother's room, all thoughts of the resuscitation efforts going on twelve feet away were gone.

Tom was surprised at how much she looked the same as she had in the Emergency Department. Her head was wrapped in bandages, and more IV bags of various sizes were hanging from hooks in the ceiling. Other than that, she looked the same. She wasn't responsive and seemed very small in the bed, surrounded by lifesaving equipment. Reaching down, he took her hand again; it was still cold but not as bad as it had been five hours before.

"Mom, can you hear me?" He said to her, but there was no response.

Linda stood across from him on the other side of the bed. At one time, Tom focused on her, and all she could do was shake her head. When she did, Tom felt crushed.

After about ten minutes, a tall, thin, dark-skinned woman approached. The name tag on her lab coat said V. Koptin, MD. As Dr. Koptin entered the room, she introduced herself. "I'm the attending neurosurgeon on Debra's case. Doctor Mounard assisted me, and I understand he filled you in on her procedure?"

"Yes, he did," Tom answered.

"Following the procedure, we did another CT scan, and

there's no additional bleeding. However, the findings of the scan indicate there was significant brain injury from the increase in pressure. At this time, we don't think this injury is something she can recover from."

When Tom didn't respond, Linda asked, "Are you saying she's brain dead?"

"We'll let her rest tonight and recheck her in the morning. But at this time, that's what we believe. Tomorrow we'll talk some more about options. Unfortunately, it's improbable her condition will improve beyond where she is right now."

They both nodded, not knowing what more to say. The doctor continued, "Visiting hours are for two more hours. You're welcome to stay with her until then. If you have any questions, I'll be at the nurse's station for a little while." She waited several seconds in case they'd anything to say and then quietly left the room. Linda moved to the other side of the bed and took her grieving husband's arm. This physical contact broke Tom's trance, and he said, "Let's go home."

Linda was surprised, "Are you sure you want to leave?"

"Yes. There won't be more information until tomorrow, and I want to get out of here." Together they left the room, turned, and headed for the elevator. Neither spoke on the way down. There wasn't much to say, and they were both exhausted from the stress-filled day. As they crossed the sky bridge to the parking garage, Linda led Tom to where she'd parked. As they got in, Tom said, "My car's at the Institute. If you drop me off there, I'll meet you at home."

"It's very late. Are you sure you don't want to wait until tomorrow to get it?" She responded.

"No, please, let's go and get it, and then we won't have to worry about it later."

Twenty minutes later, they arrived at the Institute's parking lot, and Linda parked next to Tom's car. "My keys are on my desk; I'll be a few minutes. I'll meet you at home." Leaning forward, he gave her a quick kiss.

"Don't be too long. I want you home with me." Linda said. She thought that if somehow her mother-in-law died tonight, she didn't want Tom to be alone driving when the hospital called him.

"I won't be. I'll only be ten minutes behind you." Tom replied as he climbed out and headed for the building, pulling his access card from his pocket. He knew where his keys were sitting on the desk. He could be in and out in two minutes. However, Tom knew what he needed to do, and it would take a lot longer than two minutes.

His mind was so preoccupied that the other vehicle in the lot at this late hour didn't register with him.

The door clicked open, and Tom entered the lobby. He was focused on his plan and didn't notice someone else sitting against the wall.

"Hey, Tom," Paul said.

Tom spun around, almost tripping, "Paul. What are you doing sitting down here?"

"I have been waiting for you. Come and have a seat. Tell me about how Debra is doing."

Tom reluctantly went to the chair next to his friend. He sat quietly at first, and Paul patiently waited. Finally, Tom said, "The surgery went okay. But they say she probably will never wake up."

"I was afraid of that. Tom, I'm very sorry." Paul said.

Tom again sat quietly for almost another full minute before saying. "I know why you're here. You won't stop me."

Paul nodded. "It was easy for us to say what would and wouldn't be appropriate uses for our invention when we had those conversations. Those rules don't look so important at a time like this."

"I know. It might be wrong, but it's what I have to do. Do you understand?" Tom asked.

Paul nodded, seeing the tear run down his conflicted friend's face.

"Are you going to try to stop me?"

Paul smiled gently and answered, "No. Clyde is already powered up, and the matrix has been run. It's ready to go. He'll take you back twenty-four hours."

Tom sighed, feeling as if a heavy weight had been removed from him. He hadn't wanted to argue with Paul. It was great to know, like always, Paul was there for him.

"Thank you. I'm glad you understand." Tom said as he stood.

Paul rose with him, and together they headed for the escalator. As they walked, Paul handed Tom an envelope. "When you get back, please put this on my desk."

Tom glanced at the sealed envelope and saw the letters QC on the front.

Paul explained, "I want to know what we did and why. In the future, there will be more discussions about the ethics of this technology, and I don't want this situation to be lost."

Tom entered the lab with Paul following. Walking past Clyde, who was sitting in the center of the room, Tom went to the row of computer consoles and studied the configuration of the matrix. He scanned the readouts for less than a minute, then took his cell phone from his pocket and placed it on the work table. He then disconnected the cables from Clyde and sat on the modified utility cart. Glancing up at Paul, who gave him a thumbs up, Tom returned the gesture and pressed the button. Instantly the room was darker, and Paul was gone.

Tom got off Clyde's seat and went to the desk. He picked up the phone and dialed his cell number. He soon heard his own voice on the other end of the line. "Hello?"

"QC," he then paused before continuing. "Do you understand?"

He heard the voice on the other end say in an unsteady voice, "Yes."

"Do you know who this is?" The Tom in the lab asked.

"I think so."

"Tomorrow, first thing in the morning, you must stop at Mom's house and shovel the snow and ice. Do you understand?"

"Yes, why?"

"Make sure it gets done well before she leaves for work. Don't worry about waking her."

"Okay. Is mom hurt?"

"If you do this, she won't be. Goodbye." Tom hung up the phone, sat back in the seat, and pressed the button.

When he returned to his current time, Paul wasn't there. In this altered reality, he had no reason to be at the institute at this hour.

Taking his cell phone off the table, he dialed his mother's home number. When she answered, and he heard her voice, he felt a tear running down his cheek.

Tom shut down the systems and returned Clyde to his usual place in the corner. As he walked to his office to get his jacket and keys, he stopped at Paul's office to set the envelope Paul had given him on the desk.

Chapter 21

SEVERAL MONTHS LATER, TOM ENTERED THE LAB. THE morning sun was shining through the rows of skylights in the ceiling. Paul was at a large worktable near the center of the room. He was speaking with several technicians and inspecting the device on the table in front of him. It was a steel-covered object measuring about a foot and a half wide, two and a half feet tall, and six inches thick. Tom saw several removable access plates and a few recessed controls. On the back were three sets of straps, two for over the shoulders and one for the waist. There were pads built into the back, apparently to improve comfort. As Tom looked on, Paul lifted the unit and slipped it onto his back.

"Oh, this is heavy," Paul commented, "and stiff too."

"I know," explained the younger of the men at the table. "Most of the weight is batteries."

"How much battery life is there in this now?" Tom asked.

"We were able to decrease power consumption by about eighteen percent. There should be enough battery power in the unit to remain in an alternate time for about a week before having to return and still have a comfortable reserve."

The lab doors slid open, and Catherine walked in. She approached the group while inspecting the device on Paul's back.

"Hi, Catherine. You're just in time to see the new units. They seem a bit heavier than we expected," Paul said.

"They're physically smaller than I thought they'd be," she responded.

Each put a backpack on and spent some time checking out their mobility. They found they had to fasten the straps tightly to keep the devices from sliding around on their backs.

"So, when will these be ready for their first use?" Catherine inquired.

"We want to run a few more tests on them, but by Monday, they should be ready to go," The technician explained.

"Good, because we're going to need to do some reconnaissance before we can do much more work on clothing and personal possessions from that time period," Catherine announced, speaking in Latin.

The technician seemed confused by the sudden change to a strange language, and Tom and Paul each had a perplexed look on their faces for a few moments before catching on.

"We're going to wear these around for a bit," Paul told the technician before leaving with Tom and Catherine on his heels.

The trio reached Paul's office before speaking, and as soon as they entered, Tom said, "What do you have in mind?"

"It's quite simple, and I should have thought of it sooner. The only examples of garments from this time period are museum pieces that have undergone two thousand years of aging. There are lots of guesses and assumptions, some strictly originating in Hollywood. No one alive has witnessed human interaction from that time, and the dialects of their languages could well have evolved from then to what I've learned. Before trying to interact with them, we need to spend some time studying them. If we don't do this, we probably will, at the least, draw unwanted attention. Possibly, we'll be blatantly out of place."

There was a long moment where no one said anything. Then, Tom inquired, "Do you have a suggestion to fix this?"

"Actually, I do. We need a brief scouting trip. We go back for about twenty-four hours. We arrive at night, stay near a smaller village and observe from a distance. Unlike the actual trip, our goal is to get in and out without being detected. We film the interaction of the people. We get lots of photos of clothing and, if possible, even bring back a few garments."

Paul nodded, "I see your point, but there are additional risks created with a second trip."

"Those risks are minimal compared to the ones we'll face if we go back, and it's apparent to the people that we don't belong. Our only risk is of being detected, and for that to matter, we'd have to be captured. When we're there, if we detect a problem, how long will it take to leave and return here?" She asked.

"It should only take the system about five seconds to prepare, and say another five seconds for the word to spread among the team members. If there's equipment to retrieve, or if you have been seen and need to get concealed before vanishing, it could take a bit longer," Tom said.

"We have been through the training on camouflage and concealment; I say we bring the instructor back here for another day of training and go over a few things we might want to do differently since we need to remain completely unobserved for a day," Catherine proposed.

"Alright," Paul resigned. "I'll set it up."

"Great! How long until you think we can do this?" She inquired.

"Maybe a week. That'll depend on when we can get the

instructor here, and we need to finish testing out these pack units. We need to run them through three or four smaller jumps, assuming we don't find any problems," Tom interjected.

Chapter 22

IN AN INSTANT, EVERYTHING CHANGED FOR CHARLIE BAKER. Something was very wrong. He became aware he was falling, and almost instantly was pulled underwater. Charlie was being dragged deeper by a two-hundred-and-fifty-pound equipment cart strapped to his waist.

Sinking quickly, Charlie raced to figure out what had happened. Reaching for the console, hoping to press the button and return to his time, he saw that the panel was dark. The power shorted out the instant Clyde dropped into the water.

As he got deeper, his hands grasped the seatbelt holding him in place. He'd almost chosen not to fasten it, but the last minute had changed his mind. He'd heard it wasn't necessary, but he'd been a little nervous.

Charlie felt his ears pop, and there was water entering his nose. He then felt the cart rolling backward, moving him to the highest point on the sinking mass. Then he hit the bottom and rolled over again. Now he was upside down.

Thrashing in panic, his lungs burned, desperate to breathe air. As his thrashing increased, so did his heart rate, which now passed one hundred and sixty beats per minute. His heart desperately tried to circulate blood that no longer contained enough life-sustaining oxygen.

Pulling on the strap with all his strength, he found it wouldn't give. As he attempted to scream, water rushed into his mouth.

His strength was rapidly fading as his hypoxic brain began to slow down. Finally, his oxygen-starved lungs overrode his brain. He knew he needed to hold his breath, but he couldn't help it and inhaled lake water. At the same time, his weakening hand slid and made contact with the simple plastic clasp of the seatbelt. His fading mind recalled the clasp's design, and with a tremendous effort, he squeezed the two tabs, and the belt separated.

Using the last of his strength, he pushed off with both feet from the side of the cart and started to rise. His clothes and shoes were soaked and weighed him down, considerably slowing his upward progress.

Filled with new hope, he managed to push off the shoes and then was able to kick his feet a little. As the last of his consciousness was about to flicker out, his head broke the surface, and he tried to inhale. It was an intense battle. The water in his lungs interfered with the air he needed to pull in. He coughed continuously. With every breath, he fought to pull in air while keeping his head above the water's surface. He could pull in a little more air each time he coughed up more water.

Unable to control it, he vomited and brought up lots of lake water and partially digested food. Fortunately, he hadn't eaten since lunchtime, and his stomach had been mostly empty.

For several minutes he focused all his strength on keeping his head above the surface and pulling in as much air as possible. However, the non-stop coughing used up his energy faster than he regained it.

He needed to get out of the water, rest, and determine

where he was. To one side, the shore was only about forty yards away, and he started moving towards it. His progress was slow, and he wasn't sure if he'd make it. Spotting a massive tree that had fallen into the water, he made his way toward it. The tree was much closer than the shore, and he didn't think he could make it all the way to land.

Charlie felt his body make contact with the smallest branches and grabbed at any he could, feeling comfort in their touch. He worked his way to bigger limbs that could bear his weight, or so he hoped.

With a massive effort, he pulled himself up and got most of his body out of the water. There was a bifurcation of two sturdy-looking branches, and he lay across it. He let the branches support his weight. With his legs still in the water, he closed his eyes and tried to rest. However, the coughing didn't stop, and he could feel the water had settled into his lungs. As he lay in the downed tree, he tried to determine what had gone wrong.

He'd seen some of the more senior people input the data into the computer. There were only two parts to the quantum formula. How far back in time you wanted to travel, and where to appear geographically. Charlie felt confident he got the location correct because he wanted to remain at zero. That meant the exact location where he'd originated. Therefore he should be at the Kingsman Institute, not in a lake or pond. He knew it wasn't the ocean because the water wasn't salty.

Charlie wasn't as sure about the time because he'd been unable to get the computer to format his data to calculate the time equation. Whenever he watched the others do it, they had the computer do it for them. He knew that manual entry was possible, so when he couldn't get the data sequence formatted for the computer to accept it, he entered it by hand.

He'd assumed that if he made a mistake, he could snap

back to his time and try again. He'd not considered he might appear over a blasted lake.

Charlie understood he needed Clyde's onboard computers to get him back. From the bottom of a lake, they'd be useless. Wherever he was, he was in trouble and stranded. He needed to find a hospital and get on antibiotics before pneumonia developed. Then he needed to go to Kingsman and confess to Paul and Tom what he'd done. He was also unsure how being displaced in a different time might cause problems in the overall timeline. He had to ensure he didn't accidentally change something which would impact the future. Since he was only trying to go back six days, he felt confident he could figure out the right time to approach them and undo this mess.

Lying in the branches, he rested and slept as best as he could, all the while shivering from the cold and coughing.

He awoke to sunlight starting to shine and worked his way along the tree trunk until he could jump down to the solid ground. When he did, he felt a jagged stick penetrate his sock and into the arch of his foot. Screaming and cursing, he leaned against the trunk of the tree. The scream kicked off a whole new round of heavy coughing. When the coughing subsided, he peeled back his sock and examined the puncture wound. He wasn't sure how far he would have to walk, but it wouldn't be pleasant without shoes and with a wounded foot.

As he moved away from the lake, he found a path running from left to right. Unsure of which way to go, he went to the left. He planned to listen for cars and hopefully find a road where he could hitch a ride.

After several hours of walking, the air started to warm, and as it did, his clothes began to dry, and his shivering stopped. As he walked, he thought about his situation.

His plan had seemed like a simple answer. Go back and provide himself with the lottery numbers. It sounded like a simple way to get the credit card debts paid. Now, it was looking like a big mistake. He wasn't sure where he was, but he knew this situation was terrible. Also, he'd destroyed Clyde and knew Paul would be furious.

The pain in his feet was excruciating as the sun rose higher, and the limping from the injured foot was causing knee and back pain, but he continued.

Eventually, the path intersected with a narrow dirt road. Again he turned left and followed the trail. In less than thirty minutes, he heard a sound and turned to see two men approaching on horseback. He moved to the side and waved as they arrived. As they got close, Charlie felt his skin chill and a deep fear develop. The way they dressed wasn't what he'd been hoping to see. One was tall with a mustache, and the other was shorter and thin. The smaller one appeared to be little more than a teenager. Both wore long black coats.

"What are you doing out here all alone?" The older of the men asked.

"I got lost yesterday and ended up having to spend the night in the woods. I need help getting," Charlie paused, trying to figure out how to finish his sentence, "back to town," he finally concluded.

"You can ride with me. We're headed back there now," The small one said.

"Thank you. I'm grateful," Charlie said as he struggled awkwardly to climb up onto the back of the horse and get into position.

"What's the matter? Haven't you ridden on a horse before?" The older said while laughing.

"I injured my leg in the woods. It's stiff and not moving well." That excuse appeared to be sufficient, and they dropped the topic.

"What kind of clothes are those? I never saw fancy clothes like those," Charlie's riding partner asked.

Charlie felt mild nausea return when he heard the question. His suspicions were now all but confirmed, and they weren't good.

"I took a trip to New York last year. These are new styles from Europe. I haven't been impressed with them." Charlie explained, hoping the lie would hold up.

"They don't look very sturdy or warm."

"That's what I don't like about them. I wouldn't buy them again."

As they rode on for a while, Charlie tried to avoid conversation. The whole time he was terrified as to what he'd find once he arrived.

Finally, the trees parted, and they could see a sizeable town ahead. At once, Charlie knew he was doomed.

The town had no sign of motor-powered traffic and nothing to indicate there was even electricity.

After a few minutes, he couldn't wait any longer. Even though he knew it would make him sound like a lunatic, he said, "What year is it?"

"What year? Are you alright in the head?" The man in front of him asked.

"Please, what year?" as he spoke, his anxiety increased.

"It was seventeen forty-two, last time I checked. Is that okay with you?"

"Sure"

"You don't sound too happy."

"There won't be antibiotics for almost another two hundred years," Charlie explained.

Charlie had always enjoyed history and remembered the treatment for conditions like pneumonia was usually bloodletting in the seventeen hundreds. Draining blood from the sick has since been proven to have no medical value. When the symptoms of pneumonia started, he'd be best off to avoid doctors.

"What is an antibiotic?"

"Sorry, just a joke. A terrible joke."

Chapter 23

THE FOLLOWING MORNING PAUL WAS SITTING IN HIS OFFICE studying something on his computer when Tom stuck his head in and asked. "Do you know where Clyde is?"

"Clyde? Where would he be?"

"I don't know, but he seems to be missing," Tom explained.

"Last I saw, he was sitting in the back corner of the lab. Where would he have gone?"

"It looks like someone might have taken him for an unauthorized trip."

Paul jumped up from his desk, his face turning red. "Who did? Where would they have taken him?"

"I don't know yet. Abby met me in the lab when I got here and told me. When they arrived, Clyde was gone, and his data and power cables were on the floor. We're searching the computer logs, looking into what happened."

Paul was shaking his head as he headed toward the lab. "Come on. I want to know what is happening!"

The two of them marched into the lab. Paul yelled as he entered. "What do we know?"

"Someone set up and ran the quantum matrix last night at

1:37 AM. I need to dig into the system and get you details. It'll take about a half hour, maybe forty-five minutes, to get the complete picture," Abby said.

Paul thought a minute and then said. "If someone took Clyde for a trip, they should have returned here just seconds after they left. It doesn't make sense they're still gone."

Tom nodded his agreement, went to the counter, and picked up a phone. "Lucy, I want a list of all employees who are missing from work today. Start with the technical team." After listening for a moment, he replied. "As soon as you can. Page me when you have it."

Abby spoke up from the console where she was working. "I already called the Chief of Security. I told him you wanted all last night's video and card access data. We'll have it soon."

Tom and Paul gave each other a quick glance. Both were impressed with Abby taking the initiative.

"Well done," Paul managed to say despite his fury.

Paul proceeded to schedule an all-staff meeting for 11 AM but later rescheduled it for 130 PM as more and more information came out.

THE STAFF GATHERED and sat nervously while waiting for their leaders to arrive. When they did, they could tell Paul was furious. He stood by the door but was soon pacing.

Catherine stood in the back of the room. She wasn't sure of her place here but knew she should be present.

Tom stood at the podium and spoke. "People, we've got a big problem. We rescheduled this meeting from earlier because we started digging and have found this isn't the first case of unauthorized use of the equipment."

Tom had to pause because of all the whispered conversation which broke out. When it slowed, he continued. "I'll start at the beginning. Four months ago, someone entered this facility in the middle of the night. This person kept his face concealed, but we're fairly sure who it was. They used a forged access card and briefly jumped with Clyde, going back three or four days. While there, the cameras pick this person up, leaving the lab and doing something at the desk which Bruce Wilson was using. After that, they returned to their current time. This person did a good job of deleting the data from the trip. We probably wouldn't have known anything about it if it weren't for the investigation into last night's incident."

Tom stopped to make sure everyone was following before continuing. "In the days between that unauthorized trip and the date that person went back to, a winning lottery ticket was sold six miles from here. I assume most of you remember when that happened. Everyone was talking about that all over town for a week. The day after the unauthorized trip was made, Bruce resigned from his position. Since then, I've heard rumors he came into some money."

Several heads in the room nodded as Tom spoke.

"Now, we come to last night's incident. Everyone was thought to be gone for the day by ten-thirty pm, but at 1:30 AM, the cameras pick up Charlie Baker exiting the second-floor men's restroom. He goes to the lab and gets to work setting Clyde up. He then spends over thirty minutes setting up the quantum matrix. This is something he has assisted with but has never done himself. The cameras record him hopping on the cart and disappearing. He never returns.

"We aren't sure what his exact intentions were but there was another large lottery jackpot drawn the other night that had no winner. We suspect, like Bruce, he intended to appear here in the lab in the past. It looks like he messed up the calculation. He did return to this exact location, but almost two hundred and fifty years in the past," Tom again paused to see if anyone was catching on.

Finally, Roberta, in the center of the room, gasped as the light came on for her. Whispering started all over the room as a few other people caught on.

"That's correct. The city built the Mill Street Dam about eighty years ago. Before then, this spot used to be a large pond. When Charlie popped into that time frame, he'd have arrived in about twenty feet of water. Clyde would have immediately sunk, shorted out all his systems, and lost the path back to this time."

"The computer shows the link to Clyde was lost as soon as he arrived at his destination. If Charlie didn't drown, he probably was stranded in a time before the Revolutionary War," Tom explained.

Paul couldn't sit back any longer and faced the audience. "This equipment isn't toys! It isn't for personal gain. Charlie was probably killed. An essential piece of equipment that costs nearly ten million dollars to develop is lost. The credibility of the work we're doing here is at risk. If Charlie were here, I would choke the life out of him! I can't file suit against Bruce without disclosing our work here and admitting it could be used for immoral gain.

"If anyone else is considering trying something like this, forget about it now! New security procedures will be in place immediately, and others are coming. If anyone here knew what either of those men was doing and didn't report it, you should resign now. If we can prove someone knew something and didn't report it, you'll be terminated!" Paul had been getting louder and louder as his rant went on. Turning, he stomped out of the room.

Those gathered sat in shock. They'd never known of Paul to yell at anyone before. Everyone would be avoiding him for several days.

Chapter 24

CATHERINE LEFT THE OFFICE SHE WAS USING AT THE KINGSMAN Institute. As of lately, she was spending at least as much time there as she'd been at her office at the university. Last night she hadn't gotten as much rest as planned. She'd been restless, with one thought after another entering her mind. She had a meeting at work later this afternoon, which she couldn't miss. Before that, she'd get to spend twenty-four hours in the past.

She was still sometimes surprised at her new thought process when it came to time travel. She proceeded down the hall and got a few amused looks. The amusement didn't come because of the cumbersome metal backpack unit she wore. Everyone had gotten used to seeing her walking around under its load. Today's amusement came more from her clothing.

Catherine wore military surplus camouflage fatigues. These specifically had a mixture of shades of tan and gray intended for use in desert environments. A floppy hat with a soft brim and the same camouflage pattern on it completed her outfit.

She entered the lab, walked to the side table, and checked her equipment bag. She'd looked it over several times the day before but still felt the need to recheck it. Next, she took the tan military web belt and reviewed its contents before fastening it around her waist. She drew the M26 Taser pistol and confirmed the batteries were fully charged. As she was re-holstering the weapon, Paul and Tom entered dressed similarly. By the looks on their faces, she could tell she'd not been the only one to sleep poorly last night.

"You guys look like you didn't get much sleep either," she said.

"No, for some reason, I had a lot on my mind," Paul responded sarcastically.

As the men finished checking their equipment, Catherine removed the backpack and set it on the floor. She stretched the power and data cables over to it and plugged them into the two receptacles on the left side of the unit. Within a few minutes, the other two had done likewise.

While the backpacks were getting their batteries topped off and the needed data was uploaded to their internal computers, the three time travelers anxiously waited. Paul restlessly paced the room, Tom rechecked his equipment bag, and Catherine stretched out on the floor with part of her equipment bag under her head. She tried for a couple of minutes. However, she couldn't get comfortable and soon found herself pacing the room too.

Within half an hour, the rest of the team members had arrived, and the computers had completed their calculations. They put the packs back on, and one of the technicians came around and unhooked the power and data connections. Electrodes were attached to their chests and backs in two locations. The wires fed back to the computer in the backpack and concealed beneath their clothing.

The possibility of modern equipment contaminating the past was a huge concern. If a backpack was removed or the wearer killed. The system would sound an alarm for twenty seconds. Four thermite charges within the equipment belt and backpack would be triggered if the alarm wasn't manually silenced.

Thermite is a mixture of powdered aluminum and iron oxide. When ignited, it produces massive amounts of heat.

Under ideal conditions, an ordinary hydrocarbon-based fire can produce, at most, temperatures close to 1525 degrees Fahrenheit. On the other hand, thermite can produce temperatures in excess of 4500 degrees. If the thermite charges detonated, they'd incinerate all the equipment the wearer had on their person, along with the time traveler's body.

The trio stood in a tight circle with their backs together. They were each handed a headset with a small microphone attached. These were connected to the backpacks. After each of them tested the communications sets and confirmed they were in working order, they strapped on their night vision goggles.

"Is everyone ready?" Paul asked.

Everyone agreed they were ready and got into a crouched position. Upon arriving, the team wanted to be sure they were unnoticed. The trio could run or drop flat depending on what they encountered upon arrival. If needed, they could quickly press a button and be instantly yanked back to their own time.

Tom spoke, "On three. One, two, three."

When he reached three, they each depressed a recessed button at the base of their pack.

They heard someone call out, "Good luck!" and then they were gone.

Chapter 25

ONE MOMENT THEY WERE IN THE LAB, AND THE NEXT, THEY found themselves crouched on a patch of hard earth. They'd appeared on a flat of ground between several houses. They remained crouched, not moving for about twenty seconds. When they were sure they'd arrived un-noticed, they stood and started walking. A stable was off to their left, and they silently disappeared behind it.

The smells and sounds of the animals living inside were apparent. There was also the noticeable smell of wood smoke.

"There's a hill off behind that building," Catherine whispered, pointing, "If one of us gets up there, we'll be able to see this whole side of the village."

"Works for me," Paul said. "Tom, hand over your mini cameras and microphones and head up. As soon as you're there, let us know. We'll stay here until you get up there."

It took about ten minutes for Tom to get in position. He spoke into his headset. "I'm all set."

"Ok, watch for anybody coming toward us. We're moving out now."

From his position, Tom could see his friends as they

slipped out of their concealment and began moving around the village.

It took several minutes for them to find what they were looking for. There appeared to be a small market area close to several houses. This would allow them to concentrate on this area without worrying about the entire village.

Catherine and Paul silently took miniaturized audio and video recording devices from their equipment bags and began to place them in concealed locations. Even though some of these devices were only the size of a button, they had trouble finding suitable spots to place them. Ultimately, they could only place a little over half of the ones they hoped for.

Tom's voice suddenly shot through their headsets as they were finishing up. "Some kind of animal approaching from the south."

No sooner had they turned to the south than they heard the growling of a big dog. It advanced on them with teeth showing and was snarling and barking.

Paul and Catherine reacted rapidly. Their hands dropped to their equipment belts. Each pressed a small switch on a device on their belts, and instantly, the dog started yelping in pain and ran back in the direction it had come. The ultrasonic noise generators had been most impressive in their effectiveness. While none of the team had heard anything, the high-frequency sound had taken care of the dog without having to injure or kill it.

"Guys," Tom said, "you might want to get out of there. That dog made a lot of noise, and it was clear, even way up here, that he was in pain. Someone might come to check things out."

"Ok, but we still have to hide the receiver. It has to be close by. Keep watching."

"This way," Catherine said, leading Paul to the edge of the village. There was a pile of dirt and what appeared to be debris from old cooking fires.

As Catherine removed the receiver from her bag, Paul dug a small hole in the top of the pile. It was barely big enough to bury the receiver, which was about the size of a small lunch box. A little black rubber antenna protruded from the top of the pile, and Paul concealed it with a few pieces of charred wood.

The small devices would send their audio and video recordings to the receiver, which would store them on its internal hard drive. The major weakness of the devices was their limited range and short battery life. One of their most significant benefits was if the team ran into trouble and had to leave before collecting the devices, with the push of a button, all the devices and the receiver, if necessary, would instantly short out and catch fire. While the fire would be small, it would be enough to consume the devices. At the most, there would only be a blackened piece of melted debris remaining.

After they hid the receiver, the pair split up, each finding a concealed place on the outskirts of the village. The way the team was spread out, they had three different views of the village.

They each prepared their location so they wouldn't be visible but could maintain surveillance on the community. Each of the time travelers had a digital camera with a powerful telephoto lens they'd use throughout the day whenever anything of interest caught their attention.

After less than an hour, the village began to awaken. At first, only a few people started moving about, but soon the town was quite active. Merchants were opening shops, children were off to fetch water from a well, and what appeared to be a small band of hunters formed and left together.

The observers took photos throughout the morning and wrote notes about what they saw. As the day went on, the team became hot and uncomfortable. Still, they remained in their positions, photographing the interaction of the people.

Catherine was especially thrilled by this opportunity. For

years she'd studied and taught about this time period, and now she could observe this culture live and in person. Her only disappointment was that she was unable to hear the conversations from her position. Hopefully, the receivers were picking much of it up, and she'd be able to listen to it later.

As the day progressed, they found themselves becoming more and more tired. Eventually, they took turns sleeping. As evening arrived, Catherine was studying a group of children at play when there was an abrupt sound of movement heard through her headset, followed by a nearly silent curse.

Before she could react, Tom's voice came through. "Paul? Was that you? Is something wrong?"

Catherine could hear rapid breathing, and after a couple of seconds, Paul's voice came across, sounding quite stressed.

"I was asleep and just woke up, and there's a big snake right in front of me."

"How close?"

"It's about three feet from my face," came the whispered reply.

Catherine responded. "Paul, can you tell what kind of snake it is? Remember, most snakes are non-venomous here."

"It's about six feet long; I don't see a rattle on the tail."

"Most likely, it's a Whip Snake. Those are common here," Catherine reminded him.

"If that's what he is, is he poisonous? He asked.

"No, but he may still strike, and they can hit from a meter away," she advised.

"What do I do?"

"Stay still; it'll probably leave in a few minutes."

"Should he try to pepper it or use the Taser?" Tom inquired.

"No, better not anger it."

Paul responded, "My hands are far from the equipment belt. I'd have to do some serious moving to get to anything."

Paul worked to slow his breathing, and after several

minutes which seemed like several hours, the snake moved away.

After the excitement, none of the team got any more sleep. After the sun was down and the last people had retired for the night, they waited an additional hour. Then slowly, they moved from their cover and retrieved the collector and each of the tiny receivers. Before leaving, they collected a pair of shoes and a cloak someone had left outside and quietly slipped behind the barn.

Moments later, they disappeared, instantly moving over two thousand years into the future.

Chapter 26

THE DATA THE TEAM COLLECTED PROVED INVALUABLE. THE quality of the video recording was superb. The audio wasn't as good, but with some enhancement; it was relativity clear. Entire conversations were able to be followed by Catherine. Even the men found they could often follow the meaning of the dialog.

Catherine sometimes lost the meaning of a conversation despite her familiarity with the language. This wasn't wholly unexpected and was related to the dialect of the specific region and local slang. These issues were some of the reasons she'd been so adamant they took this preliminary trip.

The video was enhanced, and the villagers' mannerisms and how they interacted with one another were studied. The specific fibers in the clothing they'd taken were analyzed. Similar materials would be used to create the garments the trio would wear on their next trip. They would also copy the shoes so they had some which fully blended in for future trips. There were clear photos of other outfits, and variations of these themes would go into the final wardrobes the time travelers would wear.

"There is one thing I'm concerned about," Tom said one

morning as they reviewed some video and attempted to imitate some of the mannerisms.

"What's that?" Paul asked.

Tom picked up the cloak and slipped the garment over his head, again aware of the musty unclean aroma of the clothing.

"Even with this on, the backpacks will be visible. You won't be able to see what they are, but it'll be clear there's something under the garments."

After a brief pause, Catherine questioned, "What about simply increasing the size of the cloak? With a few well-placed seams, the contours of the backpack can be broken up."

"That won't be enough," Paul added, "The shape of the backpack needs to be streamlined, and the corners and angles reduced. The whole unit needs to be made thinner."

Catherine was surprised. "A redesign of the pack? How long will it take?"

"Hopefully not too long," Tom responded, "I want to get this adventure moving."

"I have another concern," Paul said. "When we go back, what'll we do for money? We might be able to barter some, but there won't be much we can trade. Somehow, we'll need the ability to get money."

"Actually, that one is easy," Catherine explained. "There are many online sites where you can purchase replica coins from that era. I already ordered a good selection for us. We'll rough them up a little. Shouldn't be a problem."

Tom replied, "That's great! It seems like we have most of our details covered. We're getting close to being ready!"

The group turned and left the lab. Paul smiled at his friend as they walked, "You really seem to be getting excited about our adventure."

"Very much! This trip is an opportunity no one else has ever had. We'll get to witness the resurrection of Christ," Tom responded.

"And you don't have any doubts? Please don't answer; it's because you have faith. What's the reason you are so confident?" Paul asked.

"Simple. I'm a scientist. I study all the facts and come up with a conclusion."

"That doesn't make sense. I'm a scientist. I prefer a scientific answer to the questions about where we came from."

"The way I see it," Tom explained, "as a scientist, I look at all the facts and come up with an answer. More and more scientists from all fields of study are coming to the acceptance of a creator all the time. The chances that all the billions of things required for life on Earth would line up just by chance are simply impossible.

"Think of all the things you would need, a planet at precisely the right distance from the sun, in a stable orbit, with a habitable atmosphere and water, and a hospitable climate. The planet would need to have the right resources, so if humans could magically develop, they could build our advanced society. The odds of that happening are so astronomically impossible that you would have better luck opening the box on a brand new 1000-piece jigsaw puzzle, dumping the box off a roof, and having all the pieces land in the form of a completed puzzle. Then look at the fact that over 300 prophecies about the Christ were made hundreds of years before he was born, and all of them came true. The chances of all that coming true in one person are ridiculously minuscule.

"As a scientist, I look at those two things and must conclude there had to be a creator, and Jesus must be the Christ."

As the three continued down the hall, Paul and Catherine better understood why Tom believed, even if they still didn't.

Chapter 27

THE BOING 737 BEGAN ITS DESCENT INTO NASSAU International Airport. Seated in first class were Bruce and Cynthia Wilson.

Bruce had been busy since winning the lottery and leaving the Kingsman Research Institute. He and Cynthia designed a huge house that was currently under construction. It was being built in a wealthy subdivision near the Massachusetts / New Hampshire border. This trip was their second vacation in the last couple of months, and they already had plans to visit Australia in the fall.

Bruce had wanted to hire a private jet to take them on this trip, but Cynthia wasn't fond of flying and wanted to be in a larger plane. Bruce said that she felt this way because she wanted to take many other people with her if her plane went down. She hadn't found his joke to be funny.

On this ten-day trip, they'd stay at the Atlantis resort on Paradise Island. They had the Reef Atlantis Suite reserved and were looking forward to the luxury treatment they'd be experiencing.

Bruce was looking forward to horseback riding along the beach, and Cynthia was always happy when she got to spend time at the spa. However, they were both excited to be able to do some SCUBA diving. On their last trip, they found they loved snorkeling.

When they got home, they enrolled in a SCUBA diving class and became certified as Open Water Divers. They enjoyed it so much that they enrolled in the advanced course, but the next session didn't start until after they returned home.

While Bruce did feel a little guilty because of how he won his millions, it was still the best thing that had ever happened to him. His relationship with Cynthia had grown, and they were closer than ever, mainly because they spent more time together doing things they both enjoyed.

The wheels touched down and brought Bruce back from his daydream.

"Wow, we're here almost a half hour early," Cynthia stated.

Bruce glanced at his watch and replied, "I hope our driver is here. I don't want to have to wait for him."

"If he's not here, we can take a cab. If you remember, there was a time when that was what we did. We didn't always have private chauffeurs," she teased.

"I know, I know. I just like the personal service. That and the limos always smell better than the cabs."

The plane came to a stop, and the lighting increased. Almost immediately people started getting up from their seats and anxiously waited for the door to open so they could leave the plane. Bruce pulled a small backpack from the overhead compartment and handed it to his wife. She fought with a defective zipper before getting her book into the outside pocket.

As they exited the plane, they followed the signs for Immigration. Bruce already had the form in his hand, having filled it out well before landing. He was hoping for a quick pass-through and not an in-depth search. While he had nothing to hide, Bruce never liked all the hurdles they had to jump while traveling. Fortunately, there were minimal questions, and they got their passports stamped and moved on to collect their luggage.

After passing through the secure area, they entered the terminal. As the couple approached baggage claim, Bruce was looking for their driver. Several drivers held iPads with clients' names, but Bruce didn't see his name among them. Their luggage was already on the carousel, so they grabbed it and headed to the exit.

"Do you want to wait for him? It could be twenty minutes or more", Cynthia asked.

"No. In twenty minutes we can be there. Let's take a cab. I'll call the service from the car and tell them we were early."

Upon exiting the terminal, they moved to the crosswalk. The couple had to wait as several hotel shuttle buses and security vehicles passed. They crossed to the next curb, where a line of taxi cabs was waiting for passengers.

Bruce held up his arm, and a green cab pulled up. He handed their luggage to the driver, who'd opened the trunk.

As the luggage was being loaded into the car, they heard someone yelling. It was a security guard. He was looking at the Wilsons and holding something up in his hand. "Hey, you dropped your passport!"

Bruce reached into his jacket and, feeling the stiff cover said, "Not mine."

Cynthia reached into the backpack through the broken zipper and felt her novel, but not the passport she'd placed there after clearing customs. Realizing the cab driver was in a hurry to get out of the loading area, she raced toward the security guard without thinking about it or looking where she was going. Instantly she was right in front of a hotel shuttle bus that was moving at about 20 miles per hour. Her move was so quick that the driver, who had been paying attention, couldn't touch the brakes until after the impact.

The front bumper struck her in the right hip, and her

body spun and folded. Her forehead shattered the left front headlight. She fell, and the front wheel traveled over her chest, crushing most of her ribs and driving them into her heart and lungs. By this time, the driver was pressing the brake peddle with all his strength. The bus stopped before the dual rear wheels of the 21,000-pound vehicle went over the body. Unfortunately, it didn't matter. Cynthia Wilson was already dead.

Chapter 28

THE FOLLOWING SEVERAL DAYS WERE A BLUR FOR BRUCE Wilson. The accident had happened so incredibly fast, and the image of Cynthia's mangled body was something he knew would never leave his mind. Then there was the hysterical bus driver. Bruce didn't even want to look at him, but now felt quite sorry for the man.

After that, it was a non-stop series of events. Starting with the paramedic's arrival, the ride to the hospital, and all the questions from the police. Everyone had been extremely caring, but he remembered little of it. At some point, arrangements were made for him to travel home with Cynthia's body.

The 4-hour flight home alone had been painful. He was exhausted from lack of sleep, and sitting alone made the horrible experience worse.

The ninety-minute drive from the airport was also difficult because fatigue was starting to affect him. At one point, he almost rear-ended the Herse, which he followed the whole way, when his attention drifted.

When they arrived at the funeral home, it was late, and the funeral director asked Bruce to come back the next day, and they'd take care of all the details.

Bruce went directly home, needing some sleep. He wanted to stop at the kennel to pick up the dogs, so their presence could offer some comfort. Unfortunately, it was too late, and they were already closed. He spent much of the ride home wishing there was a way to communicate with the two German Shepherds. To let them know their mom wouldn't be coming back. He knew they'd be confused and saddened by her absence.

The exhaustion and a couple of sleeping pills had the needed effect that night. Bruce slept deeply, not awakening for almost eleven hours.

Now here he was three days later, standing at the graveside. All the friends and family had left, returning to Bruce's house. His neighbors had kindly organized a luncheon that he wouldn't attend.

As he stood looking at the grave, the guilt still overwhelmed him. Cheating the system by traveling back in time ultimately led to his beloved wife's death. He thought about all the wealth and the home under construction and hated all of it. He never wanted to go back to that life. It was all toxic to him now. All of it was gained dishonestly and cost him the one person he cared about. As he thought about it, he knew there was one thing he had to do. There was one person who could help make things right again.

Bruce got in his Lexus and headed south, unconcerned with the people waiting for him at the house. He needed to get to the other side of the city and couldn't be late.

Bruce arrived at the Kingsman Research Institute and thought about how he'd never expected to return here. Not that it was a bad place to work. It had been exciting work, and everyone was quite nice. However, he knew he'd burned those bridges the day he made his unauthorized trip into the past.

Recognizing Paul's SUV parked where it usually was, he pulled in beside it. Bruce sat back and waited, knowing this would be a very uncomfortable conversation. Bruce wasn't sure if Paul already knew what he'd done or if he'd done a good enough job at hiding the evidence.

Almost an hour later, he saw his former employer exit the building. Bruce opened his door and stepped out. Moving slowly and trying not to look confrontational, he approached Paul. Paul kept coming and then looked up and recognized the man in front of him. An angry scowl followed a brief moment of confusion.

"What are you doing here? You have no business being here after what you did!" Paul growled.

"I just need to talk for a minute, Paul," Bruce said while raising his hands in surrender.

"I have nothing to say to you. You betrayed me and all the work we do here."

"Paul, I understand. I apologize. I really do. I truly wish I could undo what I did. I need to tell you one thing," Bruce pleaded.

"I am not interested, Bruce! Get out of my way!" Paul yelled as he brushed past the other man and reached for the door of his Explorer.

In a quieter voice, Bruce said, "My wife is dead. Cynthia is dead, and it's all my fault. It would never have happened if I hadn't gone back in time and bought the lottery ticket. She didn't even know I was planning to do it. She was innocent and is now dead because of me." He had to fight to finish his statement as the tears returned and his voice cracked.

Paul hesitated briefly. He'd met Cynthia at the company picnic, and she seemed nice. He remembered she and Michelle had talked for a while, and Michelle had liked her too. After a pause, he opened his door and got inside. Before closing the door, he glared at Bruce. He wanted to slam the door and drive away, but his curiosity wouldn't allow it, so he asked. "What happened?"

Bruce gave a quick recap of what had happened, deciding that Paul was in no mood for a more extended version.

"What is it you want me to do?" Paul asked.

"Please go back. Save her. I don't care how. Warn me not to take the last vacation, maybe even warn me not to change the past and get rich. I was a good employee. Keep me from making this one mistake. I don't care. Just save her."

Paul shut the door, started the engine, and put the SUV in reverse. With his foot on the brake, he lowered the window. "I'll think about it. I'll do something. I need to think of how to do it." Without another word, he closed the door, backed out, and drove away.

Paul thought about it for the whole ride home. He eventually decided what to do. He'd make the entire mess disappear by leaving his past self a note. He'd make sure he never hired Bruce, then none of this would happen. But he wouldn't do it right away. He was in no hurry to end Bruce's pain.

Chapter 29

THE RAIN WAS FALLING HARD, AND AS TOM DROVE, HE FOUND it difficult to see what was in front of him. Slowing even further, he continued around the last bend in the road before approaching the parking lot of the Institute.

It was early, and the sun hadn't yet started to appear over the horizon. The darkness added to the poor visibility.

After he parked, he sat in the car, hoping for a break in the weather. After waiting several minutes, he decided there would be no reprieve from the drenching he was about to endure. While sitting there, he thought about what the day held for him. Sometime tonight, he'd return to this car and head home. Before that happened, he'd spend eight days in the past witnessing the most important event in history. He was extremely excited but, at the same time, nervous. The travel back in time wasn't what made him nervous. Nor was it the interactions with people from a different culture who didn't speak his language.

While he was incredibly excited to see the Lord Jesus in person, he couldn't say his nervousness came from that imminent encounter. For as long as he could remember, he'd trusted his Bible by faith and faith alone. He accepted that any misunderstandings of the scriptures would be made clear upon death. He never worried about his religion being false. He truly believed, and only in death would he discover exactly how God had designed everything. But in the next few hours, he'd go back in time to see it all for himself. What if Christ didn't come out of the tomb? What if the disciples returned in the night, as the Pharisees had claimed, and took the body?

Those thoughts were the actual cause of Tom's nervousness. Tom knew it, and it caused him to feel great shame. He'd never experienced these kinds of doubts, but they were flooding his mind now. Tom took a few minutes to pray, asking God to remove the doubts and fears from him, and found he was feeling better. But Tom knew the feelings would return if he didn't stay busy. This wasn't the first time in the last few days he'd experienced these thoughts.

Tom grabbed his laptop case and dashed from the car, snapping the umbrella open as he moved. A part of him wanted to allow the rain to give him a good soaking. It had been two weeks since his last shower. He hadn't even used deodorant during that time. His family, at first, had teased him about it, but in the previous week, they'd kept their distance.

Only in the last century had daily bathing become a routine practice, and two thousand years ago, it was common to bathe far less frequently. Smelling unusual wasn't good for people who wanted to remain unnoticed in a foreign culture. So to help blend in with the people of that era, Catherine had recommended a no-bathing plan for two weeks before the trip.

As Tom raced into the building, he was aware of headlights behind him. Not until he was inside did he turn around to see Paul's vehicle pulling in. Tom waited for him to catch up, and they proceeded to the escalator together. A team briefing was scheduled for seven AM in the conference room, but the two of them had almost an hour before that began.

Paul was the first to speak, "So, how much sleep did you get last night?"

"Not much. An hour here and a half hour there. I kept waking up."

"Same here. I was tossing and turning so much; I finally went to the couch so Michelle could sleep."

Tom nodded his understanding, "Is Michelle coming here to watch?"

"Yea. I explained there isn't much to watch, but she's wanted to see how this works for a while. I've kind of been putting her off, but I guess it's time. Will Linda be here?"

"Yes. I don't think I could have kept her away if I'd wanted to."

"I know what you mean," Paul replied. "Are you going to your office for a while before we begin?"

"Just for a minute, I want to put this stuff down and spend a few minutes in prayer. I'm really nervous and need to get focused. I can't do any studying this morning; I wouldn't be able to concentrate on what I was trying to read."

Paul nodded understandingly, "I know what you mean. I'm a bit excited too."

"You're welcome to join me if you want," Tom offered, already knowing the answer.

There was a noticeable hesitation before Paul responded.

"No, I think I'll head over to the lab and see how the preparations are coming."

Tom nodded and headed off toward his office, calling out. "I'll meet you there in a few minutes."

As Paul entered the lab, he was pleased to see the activity level that was going on. It was well over an hour before any of the lab staff customarily arrived, but today they were already deep into the preparations for the day's activity.

He had a good team working for him, and he understood the temptation which had led to the unauthorized trips to the past. Paul hoped he'd convinced everyone else not to give in to the temptation.

Technicians were re-running diagnostic routines on the

backpack units. They were looking for anything which could be a problem.

There were others huddled around three large plastic totes. Each semi-transparent container held the equipment for the team member whose name was written on the top. Medical kits, food, batteries, weapons, and audio and visual recording equipment were all getting re-checked.

Paul was aware of a feeling of excitement that hung in the room. As he observed, without interfering, he had a definite sense of pride in his people and all the effort they'd put into making this project come together.

Behind him, there was a swishing sound as the doors opened, and Tom and Catherine entered the lab. She carried the purple coffee cup she always had with her in the mornings. "Morning, Paul," Catherine spoke as they approached.

"Are you ready for today?" Paul asked her.

"I'm as ready as I'll ever be. I think we've planned and prepared as much as possible. It's time to do this," she responded.

Tom added, "I agree; let's get this done."

"I'm surprised you're so ready to do this, Tom." Catherine said, " You're about to lose a bet."

Tom knew she was only giving him a hard time but found he didn't have a quick reply ready, "We'll see" was the best response he could come up with.

"Catherine, was your husband coming to watch today?" Paul asked.

"He wanted to, but he had to fly to Denver last night for work and won't be back for a few days," she explained.

After several minutes of small talk, Paul glanced at his watch and exclaimed, "It is time to start the briefing."

They left the lab and headed down the hall toward the conference room. When they arrived, many excited, possibly agitated conversations came from within the room. Everyone became silent as soon as they entered, and worried faces looked at them.

"What's going on?" Tom asked.

"On the podium, Tom." A voice replied, and the people assembled moved back as the team approached.

On the podium was a manila envelope. From the shape of it, there was some object in the envelope. On the outside of the envelope, there were two things. First were the messy handwritten letters "QC" in large black marker. The second was two wet red smudges which could only be blood.

Chapter 30

ABOUT TWO THOUSAND YEARS EARLIER, DANIEL, SON OF THE high priest David, awoke feeling the effects of the previous night's drinking. His stomach was churning, and his head hurt. Daniel was accustomed to waking in this condition.

Looking around the room, he saw his friends, Malachi and Stone. Stone's real name was Ameur, but everyone had always called him Stone. Daniel wasn't sure of the origin of the nickname. Personally, he believed it might have been due to his loyal friend's intelligence being only a little higher than that of a rock.

Malachi was already awake and was sitting with a bucket of water, working to scrub dried blood off his left hand and wrist.

From this distance, it was impossible to tell if the blood was Malachi's or if it had leaked out of one of the people the trio had robbed the previous evening. Many of the details of the last evening were blurred. However, Daniel could still remember the other three men who had decided to get mouthy when Stone had reached into their cart. He'd helped himself to some bread which had been visible. A fight had broken out, and in the end, the trio had walked away with several baskets of food and bulging wineskins.

Tomorrow they'd begin their return to Japha. They'd been gone from the city for almost a week, and it was time to head home. Malachi was getting married in less than a week, and this trip had been in celebration of the upcoming marriage.

There was no way for Malachi to know this one crucial fact, but on his wedding night, his new bride was to conceive a child. This child would be the distant relative of a woman named Catherine Vorte. Catherine Vorte would, over 2000 years from now, marry a man named Jeff Collins.

Their trip had been enjoyable, but as usual, they drank excessively and then got into fights. None of the three knew if their three victims from the previous night had survived the confrontation. However, all three knew that over the years, some hadn't.

As Daniel rose, he checked to ensure his blade was where he expected to find it. The short sword had been a gift years ago from Malachi's father, who gave the boys each an identical weapon as they approached manhood.

As he moved, he heard a metal-on-metal sound and saw Stone beginning to move. The sound had come from the heavy length of chain the man always carried. He'd often wear it around his waist and could remove it if needed. The chain had an iron ball with a three-inch diameter on one end. This chain was the dull man's choice weapon, and Daniel had seen the deadly accuracy with which his friend could wield it.

Daniel stepped outside and breathed in the crisp morning air. One more day of play, and then home.

Returning to the small home they'd appropriated from a reluctant elderly widow, he picked up the last wineskin and drank. Today would be a good day, he assured himself.

Chapter 31

THE ROOM WAS UTTERLY SILENT AS THE THREE STARED AT THE envelope. After several seconds, they looked at one another but still didn't speak or move.

Finally, Paul reached out and carefully opened the envelope. Inside was a USB drive. Paul took the device out and examined it. There was no label, but more blood was smudged on it. He felt a chill and mild nausea developing. He studied Tom and Catherine and saw they felt something similar. Without saying a word, he plugged the drive into the laptop and opened the media file.

From the camera's angle, they could see the recording was made in this room. There was a view of the whiteboard and the door beyond, which they'd entered.

Paul glanced away from the screen, and seven feet away, the camera which would make the recording sat on the tripod in its usual place in the room.

Paul returned his gaze to the screen in time to see Catherine move around in front of the camera. Her movements were unnatural. She was favoring her left leg, and as she turned to face them, they all gasped, except for Catherine, who gave a small scream.

On the screen, Catherine stood unsteadily; she was cradling her right arm, which faced at an unusual angle. The left side of her face was red and swollen. On the right side of her face, a considerable laceration was actively bleeding. The wound was open wide and went from her lower cheek up and across her eye. As she started to speak, her balance began to fail, and from either side of the camera, Linda and Michelle appeared and helped hold her up. Their faces were pale white, and there was a look of terror on the two women's faces.

"About two hours after arrival, we'll be heading south; you'll see three men approaching." Her speech clearly showed her mouth was causing her significant pain. There were also several teeth missing from the front. "As soon as they get close enough, they'll attack. You will both be disabled and killed almost immediately. I'll be dragged off the road by the three of them. You must avoid them or deal with them before they get close enough to attack. I escaped because they were distracted when your thermite charges detonated. They went back to the path to see what the noise and smell were, and I was able to hit my emergency transit button."

After making this statement, the two other women helped Catherine away from the front of the camera. Moments later, the video ended.

No one said anything for almost half a minute, and then hushed whispers began. Soon everyone was speaking at once.

"Quiet down and take your seats!" Paul yelled. Promptly, the noise level dropped.

Paul firmly took Tom and Catherine's arms and led them into the corridor. Paul was aware of the fear in Catherine's eyes and could understand it. He too, was rattled by what they'd watched. If he'd seen himself severely damaged and in such obvious pain on the recording, he knew he'd look as frazzled as Catherine did now.

"We decide here and now," he asked in an authoritative voice, "are we still going, yes or no?"

Tom responded, "Catherine returned to tell us how to overcome this problem. Even after taking the beating she did, she didn't suggest we abort. It was clear to me that she intended for us to continue."

Catherine's voice sounded weaker than usual, but there was no hesitation. "We go."

"Good," Paul said while placing his arm around Catherine's shoulders in a comforting way. "Keep your eyes open for additional messages. One of us may bring another back to warn us about another issue."

"But, Paul, I don't understand. The other Catherine came here and left the message; where is she now? She should still be here?" Tom asked.

Before Paul could answer, Catherine said, "She went back. If she stayed here, she'd have to deal with the suffering and healing from her injuries. Going back, she trusts we won't allow them ever to occur."

Paul nodded, "That makes sense to me. It's a smart move on her part." As he spoke, he led the group back into the room.

Immediately the room got quiet again, and Paul was aware that everyone was staring expectantly at him and his companions.

"No change in plans," he announced. The relief that swept the room was evident. Most of these people had spent years on this project. While they were all still concerned by what they'd seen of Catherine on the recording, the idea of all this work not being completed was painful.

Many on the team planned for the success of this project to catapult their careers to much higher salaries.

After a moment, the meeting began. The team reviewed the details of the plans again. Everyone needed to be on the same page. The latest diagnostic tests of equipment were displayed and examined.

After twenty minutes, everyone was satisfied there was

nothing more to review, and the meeting adjourned. Tom led the way to the lab. Upon arriving, Michelle and Linda were waiting for them, looking a little nervous and excited at the same time.

Paul hoped the rest of the staff was smart enough not to mention Catherine's warning message to these two. After brief greetings, the three adventures were each given a sealed plastic bag.

Paul led the group to the basement locker room. Inside, they stripped off all of their everyday clothes. The team placed it all into another bag to be worn again after they returned. Then they got dressed from the packages they'd received. The clothing they put on was scratchy and uncomfortable in comparison to what they usually wore. Most of the garments hung awkwardly, and it was obvious why the fashions of the past were long gone. Even a close inspection of their clothing would pass all but the most thorough examination. The only exception would be the shoes. Their shoes appeared identical to the ones they'd photographed and stolen from the past on the outside. Inside was twenty-first-century cushioning and arch support, which used modern materials, some of which were invented in the last twenty years. It was determined that this was an acceptable risk since the feet of the team would never tolerate the abuse the primitive footwear would generate.

After getting into costume, they reconvened in the lab. Taking a moment, they studied each other's outfits, looking for anything out of place. After guaranteeing everything was as it should be, they gathered the rest of their equipment. The video cameras were positioned to record everything that occurred without being visible. The team put on the significantly slimmed-down backpacks. While they preferred the fit of the redesigned units, they all noticed the weight hadn't improved.

Each wore a tattered cloak that hung loosely enough to

hide the packs. Discrete pockets held other equipment, and they each had a pouch with other supplies that they wore over their shoulders.

The team posed for a quick photo at Linda's insistence. Then the data and power connections were attached to the backpacks, and the units downloaded the final instructions and began synchronizing with each other.

A few minutes later, the status lights on the computer console and the backpacks turned green, indicating it was time to go. The team lined up back to back and crouched together as they heard the computer counting down from six.

When it reached zero, they disappeared from the lab.

Chapter 32

WHEN THE LAB DISAPPEARED, THEY FOUND THEMSELVES IN complete darkness. They'd planned to arrive at night when there would be a smaller chance of encountering anyone. Their eyes were accustomed to the light of the lab, and because of the space the devices took up, they hadn't brought their bulky night vision goggles. The three of them were back to back, looking outward in all directions, ready to react to any threat, but they were completely blind. The vision would return as their eyes adjusted, which could take several minutes. Remaining still, they listened for any sounds. Not hearing any, they waited until they could see well enough to walk safely.

As they silently surveyed their surroundings, they were relieved to see they were on a rocky embankment below a narrow footpath or road. Slowly they made their way toward the road. Once there, they again stood motionless and listened for any man-made sounds. Hearing none, Paul removed a small compass from a pouch in his belt, and after a couple of seconds, he spoke, "Okay, let's go."

The three of them started down the road toward Jerusalem. They knew if all their calculations were correct,

Jesus was to enter the city this day. Their first goal of this mission was to be in place to witness that event.

They continued towards the city, which was becoming visible off in the distance. As the morning progressed, they encountered several people traveling on the roads. This was an early test of their preparations. However, the other travelers didn't even give them a second glance. Fortunately, nothing about them was too far out of place.

As they were descending a small hill, Paul heard some voices ahead. From around a bend, they saw three men approaching. The one in the center appeared to be the leader. The others were about a half step behind him.

All three had mid-length beards. The two on the left had cloaks that looked quite old. The one on the right was about half a foot taller and seemed slightly out of place with the other two.

The men were loud and energetic. When they noticed Paul and his team approaching, their conversation grew quieter.

Paul realized the discrete body language and behaviors could easily have gone unnoticed if he weren't specifically looking for such signs. He realized they were walking into a slight breeze, limiting their options. Paul also noticed that while the men seemed to continue their conversation, one of the three would briefly look at the trio every few seconds. When the distance closed to about twelve feet, he recognized the Aramaic word for "Now," quietly spoken from the one in the center.

Daniel and Malachi drew their short swords from beneath their cloaks, and Stone pulled out a chain with a weight on the end.

The time travelers didn't speak a word but raced forward, closing the distance in only a few steps. This movement threw off the would-be attackers, who were expecting quite the opposite reaction.

As the people from the future advanced, three M26 Taser pistols appeared from under their robes and immediately fired.

Catherine and Tom struck their targets directly in the throat from a distance of fewer than six feet. The men crashed to the ground and thrashed about spasmodically. The darts in their necks and the wires leading back the weapons made them look like seizing animals on a leash. Paul's darts struck the chain that the third man was starting to swing and bounced harmlessly away.

Fortunately, Stone saw his comrades on the ground flailing about and was distracted just long enough for Paul to take another step forward. Carefully setting up the angle, he delivered a forceful kick directly to the knee of the leg, which bore most of Stone's weight. Paul had pivoted enough before kicking and was able to hit the side of the joint. There was an audible crunching sound as the strike smashed the bone and tore the cartilage. With an unearthly scream, the man toppled to the ground. A second kick struck the side of his head, bouncing it off the hard-packed road. There was no additional screaming because Stone was unconscious.

The team collected the attacker's weapons, reloaded their Tasers, and moved off. Paul had wanted to strip off their clothing to ensure the men wouldn't pursue them, but Catherine had pointed out that the traffic on this road was increasing. So they decided that putting a little distance from the incident would be far more beneficial.

As they headed down the road, they could already hear two of the men starting to move. It would be a while longer before the third did, and there would surely be much screaming when he finally did.

They'd discussed keeping some of the collected weaponry. Visible weapons would make others think twice before attacking. Still, the ancient swords were quite heavy, and the people from the future were already straining under their heavy loads.

Paul was impressed with the swords he was holding. They seemed well made, had ornamented handles, and felt comfortable in his hand.

Paul looked around to make sure they were alone. Then he left the road, went about twenty-five yards, and concealed the weapons under rocks and sand.

The encounter with the thieves had lasted less than ten seconds, and that fast, the future was changed forever.

Chapter 33

DANIEL WAS CONFUSED AND DISORIENTED, WITH THE MOST unusual numbing sensation throughout his body. There was also some pain in his throat, and when he placed his hand there, it came away with a small amount of blood. Rolling over, he tried to rise to his feet but didn't seem to have full control of his arms or legs and collapsed again. Turning his head, he looked for his friends and noticed that Malachi was also bleeding from the neck and seemed to be trying to clear his head. It appeared as if Stone was still unconscious. There was a small pool of blood by his head, and his left leg was lying in an unnatural position.

Daniel didn't understand what had happened to him. He'd seen the two men and a woman coming towards them. No weapons were visible, and the decision had been agreed upon to rob them and maybe have fun with the woman. Daniel remembered that as they'd prepared to make their move, the group suddenly closed on them, and were holding strange things in their hands. After that, he remembers a horrible sensation through his body and falling to the ground. He attempted to stand several more times before he was successful.

Once standing, he had to concentrate not to fall again as he slowly took two steps toward his friends.

Hearing a sound, he peered down the road. The trio was still visible and moving away quickly. Seeing the retreating group was carrying the swords he and Malachi so deeply treasured, as well as Stone's chain. He rushed to pursue them. His legs instantly collapsed, and Daniel fell back to the ground. He wasn't yet ready for any activity.

Daniel crawled three feet over to his friend. "What happened? Why do I feel this way?"

Malachi looked at him, his eyes having trouble focusing. "Don't know. I'm hurting and numb all over."

"Those people did something to us."

"I know, but what?"

"Not sure, but I want to find out," Malachi answered.

"They took our blades and Stone's chain," explained Daniel.

"Then we must go after them. I'm not heading home without my blade!"

"I know. We'll get our swords back. But we need to deal with Stone first. It looks like he's hurt much worse than we were."

They both made their way to their friend, who made a faint moan when they touched his shoulder.

"Did you see his leg?" Daniel asked.

"Yeah, he won't walk right again. Won't walk at all for a long time."

"I know."

Stone was slowly regaining consciousness, and the first thing he saw was his friends kneeling over him. His head hurt, and his leg felt like it was on fire.

He tried to sit up, and Malachi helped him. His leg rotated slightly to the left as he moved to a sitting position.

The explosion of pain tore through his leg. The agonizing scream erupted from his mouth before he even realized what had happened. For a minute, he thought he'd pass out, and for the next several weeks, Stone wished he could.

"We need to get him somewhere to rest and find a physician. Then we'll go and get our stuff back," Malachi decided.

"I'll make them regret doing this to us!" Daniel said.

While Daniel stayed with his injured friend, Malachi went in search of someone with a cart for moving Stone.

"I'll be back, don't move his leg."

Malachi departed at a slow run in the direction where he thought the closest town was.

While he was gone, Daniel tried to make his friend comfortable. Taking a small blanket from Stone's bag, he folded it, placing it under his friend's head.

When Stone did regain consciousness, he encouraged him to drink some wine.

"What happened to me?" Stone asked.

"We were going to jump two men and the woman with them, but they attacked us first."

"I remember seeing you and Malachi falling to the ground, and then I was falling."

"One of them took out your knee," Daniel explained.

"It hurts real bad. How does it look?"

"It is all messed up, my friend. Malachi went to get a cart so we can move you, but it will hurt."

"Please don't leave me!" Stone said with fear in his voice.

"I won't. I'll stay with you until we find a place for you to rest and heal."

"What about the wedding? Malachi needs to get home to get married."

"I know. I think he's going to be late getting home."

Chapter 34

THE TEAM MOVED A LITTLE QUICKER NOW, WANTING TO PUT some distance between themselves and the would-be killers.

After a few hours, they found themselves behind a donkey pulling a cart and slowed their pace.

The foot traffic on the road was getting heavier, so Paul checked to ensure the party was together. He noticed more conversation around them and was beginning to feel self-conscious. He was concerned that it may seem unnatural for them to keep to themselves and be silent.

Apparently, Catherine was thinking this as well. Tom and Paul were shocked when she suddenly started a conversation with another woman walking in their direction. The other woman was traveling with three men who were a little behind her and were talking among themselves. Paul and Tom slowed a little to hear Catherine's conversation.

"We are from the north. We've been traveling for many weeks," they heard Catherine say in Aramaic.

"Foreigners. That explains your accent. What brings you to Jerusalem today? Did you come to see the Teacher?"

"We are coming looking for work. There were difficulties back at home," Catherine said, sticking to the plan. They'd decided to claim to be foreigners but to remain vague as to the reason for their presence.

Catherine continued, "What teacher are you speaking of?" She asked, even though she already suspected the answer.

"Jesus. Have you not heard? Some say he's the Messiah. I don't know if he is, but he's amazing to listen to. I've heard he's cured the sick and even raised the dead, but I've never actually seen it. People from all over are coming to the city to see him. We were told that he and his followers would be arriving today. Many want him to be king," the woman explained.

"That's interesting," Catherine replied, "I hope my brothers will want to wait and see this teacher when he arrives."

Paul was focusing on the exchange and found it exciting to listen and understand this language of the past.

There was a sudden commotion and yelling in front of them. Paul looked forward, but not fast enough. One of the rickety wheels had come off the rear of the cart and tumbled into Paul's path. The cart crashed to the ground, and the donkey was crying out. People were yelling, and Paul's foot struck the wheel before he knew what had happened.

Normally he might have been able to prevent the fall. However, with all the extra weight he was carrying, his balance was compromised too much. He tumbled forward, the ground raced at him, and he threw out his hands instinctively. Even before the impact, he knew the error of his action. His outstretched right hand struck first. Before the rest of him landed, the sensation of the radius and ulna bones in his forearm breaking was reaching his brain. By the time his body had hit the ground, he was already screaming.

The crowd was briefly silent as they all heard the bones break.

Tom was later a little ashamed, but he found his first

concern wasn't for his friend, but instead that Paul, in such a moment, might accidentally scream something in English. Fortunately, he didn't. He screamed loud and long.

Catherine was to him quickly, "Where do you hurt?" she asked.

For a moment, Paul stared at her blankly, and then the meaning of the strange words came to him.

Keeping it simple, he responded, "Carpus."

Catherine nodded, recognizing the Latin term for the wrist. She and Tom helped him to his feet. Others tried to assist as well, but Tom and Catherine politely refused their help. Anyone touching Paul's back would feel the solid pack below his cloak.

As he got to his feet, he looked at the people watching him and said in Latin. "I'm fine, thank you."

The three of them moved off the path and found several large rocks to sit on.

Continuing in Latin, Catherine asked, "Are you injured anywhere else?"

"No, everything else is minor bruising."

Tom took the arm and exposed the wrist. From Paul's grimace, Tom knew this action was quite painful, but his friend said nothing. The wrist was already swelling. It was deformed, but the color was normal, so the blood circulation was good.

"We need to get you back. This fracture needs xrays and probably a cast," Tom said.

"No," was Paul's only reply.

Catherine stared at him, shocked, "Paul, your wrist is broken. There's little we can do about it here. If we jump back, we can either return later or leave another warning for us to receive before the jump, to warn us about this happening. Then we can make sure to avoid it."

"Let's just splint it for now; the pain is lessening. If it

becomes too bad, we can always jump back then," Paul insisted.

Tom and Catherine exchanged glances then Paul spoke. "Serious guys, I'm all right."

Tom shrugged and began looking for the materials to splint the arm.

Paul couldn't explain all the reasons for his reaction but suspected he simply couldn't deal with the idea of returning after coming so far. He knew two things: the pain wasn't improving, and the wrist was far from all right.

Chapter 35

TOM RETURNED TO THE ROAD AND FOUND A BROKEN PIECE OF wood that had come off the cart during the accident. He'd noticed it lying in the dirt while assisting Paul back onto his feet. Breaking the board further, he made it the right length, and with Catherine's help, created a primitive splint.

Paul was closely watching Tom get the splinting materials together and didn't realize what Catherine was doing until she grasped his upper arm and said: "Don't move." The cold, wet sensation of the alcohol pad was noticeable right before he saw her plunge the twenty-two gauge needle into his bicep.

"Morphine?" he asked.

"Yes, ten milligrams. Also, swallow these." She gave him several orange pills, "Eight hundred of ibuprofen too. That will help with the pain now and for several hours. It should also reduce some of the swelling. I don't want to give you any more, or you'll be too doped up to function."

"Alright, can you give me some water so I can swallow them? I can't pull it off my belt right now."

Catherine made sure no one was looking and then pulled the plastic canteen from under Paul's robe. She removed the top, and he drank enough to take down the pills.

Catherine helped hold the arm while Tom lay the piece of wood under it. While ignoring Paul's moaning, they attached it to the arm with a strip of linen.

"How does it feel?" Catherine asked.

"A bit better," Paul lied. "It will do for now."

"While we're here and secluded, we should check all the equipment and eat. It'll be difficult to eat any of the food we brought if there's anyone around. It'll look and smell different than what they're familiar with," Tom suggested.

Agreeing, the travelers dug into their rations and quickly ate. They each consumed two power bars and several handfuls of trail mix. The plan was to eventually obtain local food, or their stock would run out in a few days. There was no way to carry an entire week's worth of food and all their other equipment.

After eating, Tom collected and burned all the wrappers, ensuring nothing was identifiable.

After twenty minutes, the medications started taking effect, and Paul's face was regaining much of its normal color.

The three time travelers returned to the road and resumed their journey toward the city. After another hour, they arrived outside the city gate. A sizeable crowd had already formed and lined both sides of the road for almost one hundred yards. There was a festive mood in the area. The people were joyous, even celebratory. Everyone was talking about the upcoming arrival of the Messiah. Most of these people had heard him speak; some claimed to have seen him perform miracles.

Others had come out to see what was causing all the commotion. Some listened curiously. A few were unconvinced and wandered off after a few minutes.

While looking at the people who'd gathered, Tom became aware of the third category of people in the area. There were about eight men standing together off by themselves. Their appearance was much different. They wore fancy clothes and appeared better groomed, and stood with what Tom could only describe as arrogance. These men listened to what was said but didn't comment. Most of the other people present seemed to avoid them.

Tom could only assume these were the Teachers of the Law. Tom knew these men had already been planning to kill Jesus.

The crowd doubled over the next half hour, and the excitement grew. Word began to spread that the Teacher was almost there. The donkey he rode would be in front of them in a few minutes.

Catherine looked at Paul, his eyes were glazed, and he was unsteady on his feet. She took him by the arm and led him to the stump of an old fig tree; she eased him down until the stump was taking most of his weight. The small jagged stump must be digging into his buttocks, but at least he wouldn't pass out. She hoped he wasn't so high from the pain medications that he wouldn't remember this event. Tom had moved to join them, and she could tell he was excited about what would happen.

Catherine remembered back when she was in college. She'd gone to a campaign rally for a presidential candidate she supported. She recalled how impressive it was to see, in person, a man who would most likely become the President of the United States. When she saw Tom's excitement, she realized he was about to see a man he believed was the Son of God.

As she considered this, she became aware of the crowd becoming more animated. There was a contingent coming down the road towards them. Several men were on the road, and behind them was another figure seated on a donkey.

Catherine was almost as excited as Tom. Here was one of, if not the most famous people in all of history. Jesus was a pivotal player in the society she'd dedicated her life's work to study, and he was coming down the road. He'd pass directly in front of her. She checked to verify her garments were straight, and no folds were obscuring the buttonhole cameras that were recording this event.

As he arrived, she saw people laying palm branches, which they'd recently collected, on the road in front of the donkey. Jesus smiled at the crowd, occasionally stopping briefly to speak to one person or another. Catherine was fascinated by the loving look on his face as he talked to the people.

She was aware of someone touching her arm and glanced over to see Paul. He'd stood, used her for support, and studied the approaching figure.

For his part, Tom was staring with his mouth half open. This wasn't what he was expecting. He had an image in his mind of what Jesus would look like all his life, and this wasn't it. He didn't look anything like the photo on the wall in his office. Jesus had darker, Middle Eastern features and black hair. Certainly not the Anglo appearance he always envisioned. He was close to six feet tall, and his eyes had an intensity he couldn't explain. Jesus had a medium build and was about one hundred and sixty pounds. Otherwise, there wasn't much noticeable. His appearance was somewhat ordinary.

When he was directly in front of them, Jesus stopped the animal again. However, this time he smoothly dismounted. Holding up a hand as he did, those with him held back.

He stared directly at the three foreigners and advanced. Tom promptly dropped to one knee. Paul felt his legs beginning to weaken, and his heart was pounding.

The Teacher stopped inches from them. Looking at them, he said quietly, using clear perfect English, "You don't belong here. You must not interfere."

As he spoke, he reached out and placed his hand on Paul's shoulder. The sensation was immediate. The fog surrounding Paul's mind instantly cleared, and all traces of the narcotics were gone. At the same time, Paul felt something within his damaged arm move, and the pain instantly vanished.

Responding to Christ's words, Tom replied in Latin, "We won't interfere, Lord Jesus."

Jesus smiled, looked down at the kneeling believer, and placed a comforting hand on his shoulder.

"Stop doubting and believe," he said to Paul.

Turning around, he remounted the donkey.

As he moved on, Tom got to his feet, feeling briefly unsteady and with a look of shock on his face. He turned to the others and said, "He spoke to us. Jesus touched me; he actually touched me! The Lord touched me!"

"I know, Tom, I know," replied Catherine, trying to calm Tom's excitement. "We heard and saw. I want to know how he knew we weren't from around here. What did he mean by you must not interfere?" After a moment's pause, the most surprising detail came to her. "He spoke English! How's that possible? How would he know, too, even if he could have?"

Tom was about to respond when he was interrupted. Paul moved forward and placed a hand on Tom's back. "Tom, did you see? He touched me too."

Tom looked at Paul and responded, "He did? That's great."

"You don't understand," Paul said, pulling his other arm out from under the cloak, "Look! When he touched me, my wrist was healed!" He unwrapped the material holding the splint together and let the wood fall to the ground. He made a fist several times and rotated the wrist in both directions.

Catherine had been listening and watching as the man on the donkey continued down the road. Now she whipped around and stared at Paul's arm. The wrist and lower arm, which had been fractured, swollen, and crooked, were now completely healthy in appearance.

Is there any pain?" asked Catherine.

"None. As soon as he touched me, it healed."

"You were also weak from the pain medication," added Tom. "Is that better too?"

"Yes, it also cleared up at the same time as the pain."

Tom smiled and said, "You see, he isn't just a wonderful preacher and historical figure."

"I'm starting to think I might lose the wager," Paul said.

"I knew that from the beginning," Tom replied.

"Yeah, I guess you did."

While discussing the miraculous event, they became aware that people in the area were looking at them. Some were pointing, and others were talking among themselves. It was clear the trio was the topic of conversation.

After a few awkward seconds, a young man in his early twenties approached them. Apparently, he was the unofficial spokesman for the locals. "The teacher, he stopped and spoke to you," he said in Aramaic.

Paul replied, "Yes, he did."

"We were wondering why he stopped to speak to you. You're clearly strangers here, but he singled you out. Why?"

Paul was struggling; this man was speaking too fast for him to decipher. He was thinking it through and was reasonably sure he knew the question when Catherine said, "My friend here is from the north; his speech isn't good. His arm was injured in a fall earlier today. The Teacher must have known that. He touched my friend and healed his broken arm."

"Is this the truth?" the man inquired. His wide eyes weren't hiding his surprise.

As they spoke, Paul exposed his arm to show the man. As he did so, he felt a little foolish. There were no marks or any other evidence as to what had happened.

"Yes, it's the truth," Catherine began but was cut off by another voice.

"It is the truth," said a familiar female voice.

It was the woman Catherine had talked to on the road. "These men were walking the road with us earlier; he tripped over a wheel that had come off a cart. When he fell, the wrist broke. I saw the disfigurement myself."

The man stared at Paul's wrist. "So, what people are saying about him is true," he said after several seconds of consideration.

"Yes," Tom said, "It's true."

The conversations continued for a while before the crowds broke up.

As the last of them started moving on, the trio noticed the Teachers of the Law glaring at them disapprovingly.

Chapter 36

FOLLOWING AT A DISTANCE, THE TRIO PASSED THROUGH THE city gates and entered Jerusalem. Their priority had been to locate a place to stay, but with their target in sight, they also wanted to stay close to him.

Catherine and Paul were especially curious. Even their group's brief exchange with Jesus was enough to convince them there was more than expected going on. Neither was willing to reverse their stance on religion yet, but both knew that might change by the end of this adventure.

There were many merchants and street vendors all along the main road. Several were selling linen, others vegetables, and some had prepared foods. Various animals were available for sale, and one specific vendor was trying to sell a snake to a young couple. The area was full of different odors. They could smell cooking meat, smoke, and animal waste all at the same time.

The group followed as Jesus' party headed towards the temple, which was the primary structure in this area of the town.

"According to scriptures," Tom began. "Jesus will spend the night outside the city. He'll go to the temple in the morning. When he arrives, he'll throw out all the merchants who set up there and chastise them for conducting business in God's house. I think we can slip away now and find a place to stay. We can catch up to him in the morning."

"Sounds like a good plan to me," Paul added.

As they broke away, Paul was surprised at how willingly he'd been to accept that what the scriptures said was what was going to happen.

While walking, Catherine carefully studied the crowd. She was looking for the right person, and after several minutes, she spotted her. She was a teenage girl who was selling herbs from a basket. The other two waited within earshot while Catherine approached. "We are visitors from another city and are looking for a place to stay for a few nights. Do you know of a place where we might find a room?"

The girl replied, "My friend's father rents rooms at his inn. If you go up this road and turn left, after a while, you'll pass the theater. Just past there, you'll see a sign that says rooms for rent. Turn there, and it is the third building on the right." As she spoke, she pointed down the road.

Catherine thanked the girl and looked at the men. "Did you follow what was said?"

They both nodded, and the trio started walking.

"We are heading into the Upper City if I remember the maps correctly," Catherine explained.

It turned out to be a longer walk than any of them expected. After fifteen minutes, they were deep into the city and could see the theater ahead. To the left was a shop selling animal hides; a narrow lane was beyond it.

As they passed, two men came out of an alley and casually approached them. Both wore cloaks and had neat beards. One was shorter and looked up and down the street, while the other focused on the trio. These men didn't appear threatening, just quite ordinary.

In a friendly voice, the taller of the two said in Aramaic,

"Greetings, friends. Could we please get a minute of your time? We'd like to discuss something."

Tom and Paul were determining the meaning of what was said and were about to reply when Catherine spoke. "I'm sorry, but we're late to meet someone. Maybe later."

Catherine didn't want to get into a situation where the men's limited language skills would be apparent. Also, she assumed the intruders were merchants looking to sell them something. However, the new arrival solved that problem. In slightly accented English, the tall man spoke again in nearly a whisper. His gaze moved between Tom and Paul. "Mr. Kingsman? We need you to follow us, please."

The trio froze in place. Tom felt his heart racing. None of them knew how to respond.

Now the shorter of the new arrivals spoke. "This way, please." He pointed down the narrow alley and started to move in that direction.

The others stayed in place until Paul said, "Follow him." As they moved down the alley, Paul's hand wrapped around the grip of the Taser pistol, which he still kept concealed. Looking at Tom and Catherine, he saw that her hand was in a similar place under her garment, but Tom's hands were empty and at his sides.

They traveled about twenty yards down the alley and stopped. There didn't appear to be anyone else around.

"I assume you're Paul Kingsman and Thomas Wallace?" the shorter one said.

"And Catherine Collins," Tom added.

The two men looked at each other and seemed confused.

"What? Who's Catherine Collins?" This question was quickly cut off by the taller of the two.

"Please excuse our error. It's just a misunderstanding." He glared at his partner as he spoke. The other man became silent.

Tom spoke up, "Who are you? How are you speaking English?"

"I'm sorry. We won't be able to answer most of your questions. What we'll tell you is we're like you. We're from the future." As he spoke, he slid up the left sleeve revealing a futuristic-looking device. It was a wide wristband with numeric readouts and many small indicator lights. It appeared to be about a half-inch thick and three inches wide.

"What's that?" Asked Paul in a voice filled with confusion.

"It's similar but much lighter than those Pack2 backpacks you're wearing," He paused, smiling.

"What's a Pack2?" Paul asked.

"That's what the model of backpack used on your trip will eventually be called."

The tall man paused and then continued. "I can't tell you how far in the future we're from, but it's significantly further than your time."

"Why are you here?" asked Tom.

"We are here to stop you," he said with a grin.

"Stop us from doing what?" Paul responded, feeling his grip tighten on the Taser.

"We need to stop you from staying in the rooming house you were headed to."

"That's all? Why?" Catherine asked.

"You still don't understand how dangerous your being here is. You've already changed things here that will have permanent impacts for all of the time. Fortunately, none of the people who were changed are critical to the outcome of any major events. However, if you stay in that rooming house tonight, something will happen which will cause a change to the timeline, which will greatly alter the future."

"What do we do if we stay there, and how do you know?" Tom asks.

"We cannot answer your questions specifically. All we can say is your interference there will result in someone being born who shouldn't be. Their descendant will lead a revolt in the future, and they'll assume the leadership of a nation and completely change that nation's political direction. Millions of lives are created and destroyed. All because you stay in that rooming house," explained the shorter of the two. Speaking for the first time since his partner cut him off. As he spoke, he continued to look questioningly at Catherine.

For several seconds, no one spoke as they contemplated the situation.

Finally, Paul asked. "Is there somewhere better for us to stay?"

"We have arranged something for you. At the end of this alley is a room off to the left. We have rented it for a week. There's also food there. That should reduce how much you need to interact with the locals. It's more isolated and should give you some privacy."

"Thanks, I guess," said Paul.

"Do you have any other advice?" Tom asked.

"Did you bring money from your time?" Asked the taller of the two.

"We brought replica coins from this period," Catherine explained.

"Let me see them."

They all dug out the coins from an inside pocket in their garments and handed them over.

"These aren't too bad. Good chance no one would have become suspicious. Take these instead, they're real." As he said this, he handed over a single bag. It weighed about two pounds and was closed by a tied strip of cloth.

"Just remember, even the most innocent actions here could have serious consequences. Be careful; we don't want to have to come and guide you again." This last statement, he said with another grin.

"Sent back from where?" Paul questioned.

"From our perspective, you developed this technology

many years ago. Over the decades, it was frequently used, even after governments created strict guidelines against its use. It became clear that there needed to be a method to detect changes made to the past and prevent the ones which introduced major problems. Protocols needed to be established to guarantee catastrophic timeline changes weren't introduced. Therefore our group was formed."

"Can you tell us what else we've already done and what damage it caused?" Tom asked.

"Sorry, we aren't allowed to do that. We have stringent protocols."

His partner said, "We must be going now."

Without another word, the men from the future reached under their sleeves and, in unison, without again revealing the band, activated the device and disappeared.

Chapter 37

THE THREE OF THEM STOOD LOOKING AT EACH OTHER. Eventually, Tom said, "I guess we should check out our room." And he led the others further down the alley.

While walking, Paul thought about what had happened. It made sense that if, in their time, they had this technology, it would also exist in the future. Therefore, it was impossible to know how many people from the future could be observing these significant historical events. It also made him quite uncomfortable. In the eight hours since arriving here, they'd already managed to interfere with future events and had no idea how that had happened.

He was also confused as to how staying in a rooming house could cause someone to be born who shouldn't. He couldn't believe he or Tom would get someone pregnant in the past, so did that mean they'd save someone's life? It was all very bizarre.

The narrow passage led to a rectangle-shaped room at the end of the alley. Between the alley and the room was a small area cut into the rocks with the remains of a cooking fire.

The room was about twenty feet deep and ten feet wide. A curtain served as a door to provide privacy from the alley.

Several rolled-up sleeping mats and some blankets lay in the corner. An old basket held several loaves of bread, various vegetables, fruits, and some smoked meats and fish. Next to the basket were two jugs of water and a pile of dried firewood. The only other thing in the room were a mismatched pair of wooden stools and a small table.

Tom stepped out of the room and back to the alley. After a minute, he returned. "I don't think there's anyone around. I think we can talk freely."

"Good, let's get these packs off and rest for a while. My shoulders are killing me," Paul responded.

Working together, the trio set the safety on the self-destruct device built into the packs and assisted each other in removing them. They inspected the three packs for damage and ran the built-in diagnostics. So far, everything was in perfect working order. Placing the three packs in the back corner, Catherine covered them with a blanket, and Tom propped the sleeping mats against them. If someone were to enter the room, hopefully, nothing would look out of place.

The guys sat on the stools and Catherine on the table while passing around a plastic bottle of water they'd brought with them. The bottle would be refilled from the jugs in the room later. Before doing that, purification tablets would be added to kill any parasites.

Tom spoke first. "Well, I felt good about our progress until we ran into those two."

Catherine nodded, "They made me uncomfortable. The short ones kept staring at me, and made it sound like we were reckless. The things those two claimed didn't make much sense. How would they know how a change by us had made a difference hundreds of years in the future?"

Paul agreed, "I know, but it does remind us how careful we need to be."

"I don't understand how they'd know the two of us but be confused about Catherine," Tom added.

"Something about that felt wrong. It felt like, historically, I shouldn't be here," she agreed.

"I know. There's much more to that, and I'm not comfortable not knowing what it is," stated Tom.

After a long pause, Paul added, "There was one thing good about meeting them; this room is perfect for us. It gives us the privacy we need and is near the center of the city."

They continued discussing their current situation and worked on modifying their plans. While talking, one of the loaves of bread was passed around, and each broke off some and ate it. Tom couldn't help but think about when Jesus had fed over five thousand people with three loaves and a few fish. It seemed God wasn't trying to impress them with that move again because the whole loaf was gone in a few minutes.

The last thing the team checked was their recording equipment. Paul reviewed some of what they'd recorded and found the quality acceptable.

The day was getting late, and Jesus would spend the night in the town of Bethany, which wasn't far from Jerusalem. They decided to do a bit of exploring. It was still light enough that their cameras would record well.

After resting for about thirty minutes, they got their packs on and re-armed them. All three wanted to leave them here and not have to carry them, but the risk of someone finding them was far too high.

They headed deeper into the city, making a specific effort to get close to some of the upscale buildings and record the architecture.

While the wager was their priority, the opportunity to study and bring back documentation about this time period was something all of them agreed was also of high value.

After walking for several hours, they returned to their room and slept.

All three agreed to head to the Temple in the morning to try to catch up with Jesus there. They all wanted to listen to him speak and see how the crowd responded to him. From biblical history, the team knew he'd be arriving and throwing out all the vendors who had set up shop beyond the outer courtyard and inside the holy area of the Temple.

They also planned to spend some time traveling to some of the more well-known parts of the city and surrounding area and video record as much as possible. The plan was to check out some key locations where Jesus would be throughout the week. That way should the time travelers become separated from him, they wouldn't miss a critical historical event because they couldn't locate where he was.

Chapter 38

Sara and her husband Ran had only been married a little over a month and were looking forward to the week they were to spend in Jerusalem.

Ran's father owned several vineyards and four farms about thirty miles from the city. All of them were quite profitable. His father was well respected and an elder in the community. Ran worked hard for his father and someday would inherit his properties. This would allow him to provide the best things for the family he and Sara planned to have.

The couple had traveled to the city to attend the wedding of a friend they'd grown up with. However, the journey took longer than expected. The couple planned to arrive around mid-day, but it was getting dark and was past supper time. The two of them walked along, guiding their donkey, which was carrying their bags. They'd taken turns riding the animal to rest their feet during the trip.

Their friend had recommended a place to spend the night, and they were now concerned no rooms might be left at this late hour.

Ran and his wife walked past the theater and soon saw an

inn with a sign offering rooms to rent, exactly as their friend had said.

Turning the pair soon saw the rooming house ahead.

Upon entering, they saw the manager, who greeted them with a friendly nod.

"Excuse me, sir. Do you have any rooms available?" Ran inquired.

"Yes, I do. I have one available. I was holding it. My daughter's friend told me about three travelers she sent here, but that was hours ago, and they haven't shown up. It's yours if you want it."

"Great, we'll be staying five nights," Ran handed the man six coins which he accepted and asked, "Is there any food available? We're arriving later than expected."

"There is some stew left. It's rather good tonight. After you get your things in your room, come back down. Several others are eating and drinking in the dining room. You can join them. I'll have the stew and some bread ready for you," the manager said.

"We also need a place to tie up our donkey and some feed for him. Is any available?"

"Take him out back. There's a small stable there. You'll need to pay for his feed."

Ran gave the man another coin and went back outside. Sara helped as he got their bags off the tired gray donkey and led him to the stable, where they got him some feed and water.

Returning to the inn, the couple took their belongings to their room. There was an old bed against the wall and a table. The room wasn't much, but it would be adequate. They didn't intend to spend much of their awake time here.

Returning to the main floor, they washed their hands before heading to the dining room. There was a lot of noise coming from the room. Eight other guests were seated.

A man and a woman were eating by themselves. The other

six were rather big men who were loud and drinking. The six seemed to be having a good time and greeted the newcomers cheerfully.

There were a couple of open spots at an unoccupied table, and the new arrivals sat down and only had to wait a couple of minutes. A short, stocky woman wearing an apron brought out two bowls and a small loaf of bread. Each bowl had a spoon and contained a dark broth, lots of vegetables, and some meat. It smelled good and was a welcome sight after the long journey. Ran felt his stomach rumble at the sight of the meal.

"Good thing you got here when you did. This is the last of the stew," the woman said.

"Thank you. It looks delicious," Sara told her with a smile. She was thankful they'd been told to stay at this inn. Everyone had been very kind, and the food was appealing.

As the couple began to eat, one of the loud men stood and headed towards the door. He'd been drinking for a while and was somewhat unsteady on his feet. One of his friends jokingly shoved him from behind as he started walking. The big man lost his balance and fell into the table where Sara and Ran had started eating. When he hit the table, the front leg collapsed, and the two bowls of stew went flying. One of which landed in Ran's lap.

Ran was tired and hungry, and his anger which was almost always in check, exploded. Jumping to his feet, he verbally assaulted the man who had ruined their supper and clothes.

The large man had regained his footing and was already annoyed at the embarrassment he felt from his friend knocking him into the table. Glaring at the scrawny kid who was berating him, he shoved Ran into the wall.

Ran hit the wall hard, and his back screamed in pain. Pushing away from the wall, he moved toward the bigger man and pulled the dagger from his belt.

"No!!" Screamed Sara, who knew Ran had no real fighting experience.

The drunk had pulled his own knife, and as Ran's blade sunk into his opponent's left upper arm, the larger man drove his into Ran's upper left chest. As Ran collapsed, Sara caught him and gently lowered him to the ground. By the time he was flat on the ground, his skin had already turned pale white, and Ran's breathing was struggling.

The laceration to the left ventricle of Ran's heart was causing most of the blood leaving his heart to dump into his chest cavity, collapsing the left lung. In less than thirty seconds, Ran was dead.

The assailant had been watching Ran but now turned toward his friends with an expression of pain and fear on his face.

In uncontrolled fury, Sara grabbed the knife from her husband's chest, jerked it free, and stood. With a scream like most of them had never before heard, she drove the blade deep into the man's back. He crashed to the ground, and Sara had to jump out of the way so he wouldn't land on her.

As the inn's manager ran into the room, he saw Sara on the ground, holding her dead husband and weeping fiercely. One of his other guests was on the floor writhing in pain with a knife in his back.

The sight horrified him, and then he was angered because he'd have to deal with the Roman authorities who would undoubtedly soon be arriving.

Chapter 39

THE NEXT MORNING TOM AWOKE FEELING STIFF FROM
sleeping on the hard mat. As he sat up, he was aware that the
discomfort in his shoulders from the heavy pack had only
minimally improved. Slowly he got to his feet and stretched,
trying to relieve some of the stiffness. As he moved, Paul
started awakening. Catherine was already up and stretching.

"Get some Ibuprofen in you. It should help," she
suggested.

After taking the medication and eating some of the
provided food, the time travelers began checking their equipment and prepared to head out. Leaving the alley the trio
proceeded down the road.

As they walked, Tom explained. "When we get to the
Temple, there's an outer courtyard where we can go. We won't
be able to enter the Temple itself. That's strictly off-limits to all
gentiles. Not even the Romans are permitted to enter. This
outer courtyard is often referred to as The Court of the
Gentiles."

"That is correct," Catherine added. "The penalty for
someone entering the actual temple, who isn't a Jew, is death."

A young girl walked up to them and they recognized her.

She was the one who had given them directions to a rooming house. She was holding the basket of herbs.

"I'm glad to see you're unharmed. Did you stay at my friend's place?" She asked.

Catherine replied, "No. Thank you, but we ended. up somewhere else."

With that statement, the girl looked relieved.

"Why, did something happen?" Paul asked.

"Yes. My friend said some travelers arrived late yesterday and took the last room. One of them ended up getting into a fight with another guest. They fought with knives; one is dead, and the other probably won't survive. I'd thought you might be involved," the teen explained.

"No, fortunately, we weren't there."

"I'm glad you found somewhere else." With that, she bowed her head and left to continue trying to sell her fragrant leaves.

While continuing, each thought about what had been said. This incident must be what the others had told them about. The fight would never have happened if they'd stayed in the rooming house as planned. For future events to proceed as history dictated, one or both of those men needed to die in that fight.

Paul broke the silence, asking something the others had all thought. "If just changing where we spend the night can have such a profound impact. I wonder what was changed by our battle with the three robbers on the road when we first arrived. Our future friends made it clear something was changed."

Tom added, "We'll never know. Was it that their lives were changed or were they supposed to attack someone behind us, and couldn't because we disabled them? Simply taking their weapons could have changed several future interactions they'd have had with others."

Catherine added, "Something as small as Paul tripping on

the cart's wheel could change something. Would someone else have been closer to the cart if we hadn't been there? Would that person have tripped? If so, what would their injuries have been, and how might those injuries have affected what they did or didn't do."

After a minute to think about this, Tom said. "This all kind of makes me glad we've got the guys in the future making sure we don't make any major changes."

Paul agreed. "True, but we still need to limit our interaction with the people here. We need to be, as much as possible, just observers."

After a minute, Catherine said. "I'm starting to think this technology could be very dangerous."

Not saying a word, the two men stared at each other. Both were thinking the same thing.

As the three of them approached the temple, many more people were in the area. Upon entering the outer court, they saw many well-dressed men gathered in groups and engaged in animated discussions. These men appeared to be scholars. Around the parameter of the outer court, there were numerous vendors. Many of them were selling animals for use in sacrifices. Mostly it was doves, but some had small lambs. There were other tables where people were trading coins.

"There's a tax that everyone has to pay to enter the temple, and it must be paid in Hebrew money. The more common money in this area is Roman. People can exchange Roman money for Hebrew for a steep price. Not only the money changers, but the priests who get paid from this tax, make lots of money off this," Catherine explained.

Looking around, it became clear there were so many vendors that some had set up beyond the outer courtyard and were even doing business further in the temple, beyond where they, as Gentiles, were permitted to go.

The trio walked around the courtyard, verified their

recording devices were on, then moved against the outer wall and waited, trying not to attract attention.

An hour later, some commotion occurred, and a new group entered the courtyard. There was one man out front and about a dozen right behind him. Another twenty or so followed further behind. As the group got closer, they could see that the man out front was Jesus. He was moving quickly and clearly with a purpose, passed through the courtyard and into the temple area.

Seeing Jesus again was almost as exciting as the first time. All three of them were still amazed to see such a historically prominent person right in front of them.

Almost as soon as he entered the inner temple, there was shouting, but from where Paul and his team were, his words couldn't be understood but his anger was obvious. They all had read what was to happen and knew he was reprimanding those who'd moved their booths into what was a holy place. The activity went on for several minutes. With the sounds of loud voices and items falling and being knocked around.

Eventually, the noise quieted, and the men who had set up their tables and animals in the temple quickly moved them out and started looking for space in the outer court. There wasn't enough room for all of them, and most had to exit the outer court and look for a place to set up elsewhere.

The three time travelers wandered among the crowd. Listening to what was said and recording as much as possible. There were several different opinions present among the people. Some were trying to understand why he thought he had the right to disrupt the temple business. Some were pleased he'd stopped the offenses from occurring in the temple, and the third group seemed to be the ones who were his followers and thought he was going to be the new King.

Many people were waiting for him to come back through the courtyard, hoping to see him do something miraculous.

When he emerged, none of the anger he'd displayed when

he was in the temple was evident. Taking a seat on an available bench, the people swarmed toward him.

Tom, Catherine, and Paul wanted to hear what he was saying but stayed near the back. They couldn't afford to get in the middle of the crowd and have someone press against them and feel the hard metal of their packs.

Unfortunately, this made it difficult to hear. But the trio from the future could understand that Jesus was talking about the Kingdom of God and leaving sinful lives behind. Many were asking questions and discussing Jesus' answers.

After about a half hour of his teaching, a man with a severe limp pushed his way through the group. He spoke to Jesus, but they couldn't hear what was said. Jesus touched him, and there was a gasp from the audience, and the man walked to the back, no longer limping but crying in delight. Many more people pushed their way to the front, and Jesus touched them.

The three of them had split up and were each trying to get a better view of what was taking place at the front.

As Paul circled the gathering, he noticed someone was watching him. Moving to get a better view, he felt a chill run through him.

He worked his way over to Tom, casually took his arm, and led him to where Catherine was standing.

As they backed away from the other people, Paul said, "Remember the two guys we tasered yesterday?"

The others nodded.

"One of them is here in the courtyard and was looking directly at me."

Tom responded, "There are too many people here, so he can't do anything now."

The others agreed but were left wondering what to do.

Chapter 40

WHEN JESUS FINISHED SPEAKING TO THE CROWD AND HEALING the sick, he and his disciples left the courtyard and many of the people followed. The three outsiders mixed with the group and followed along.

As soon as possible, the team broke away, moved down a side road, and waited while watching for anyone following them. Hopefully, they'd managed to slip away unnoticed. Once comfortable that no one was following them, the three went back to their room. It was now past the mid-point of the day, and they needed to eat and make plans.

Paul carefully studied the walls of the alley near their room. He spotted what he was looking for about three-quarters of the way to their room. There was a loose rock in the wall, about ten inches from the ground.

Pulling a knife from his pocket, he carefully pried it out. Then he took a small device from his inside pocket and switched it on. It was about the size of a deck of cards. It fit nicely into the hole he'd made. Paul then packed some loose dirt all around it to conceal it.

The batteries would need to be changed every twenty-four hours, but this low-range motion sensor would alert them to someone coming down the alley. If someone passed in front of it, a beeping sound would start in Paul's backpack and slowly increase in volume until silenced. Last night they'd not been too concerned, but after seeing the man watching them in the crowd, it was time to be more careful.

Once in the room, they assisted each other with the pack removal and ate the smoked meat and some of the fruits.

Tom spoke, "Any idea what this meat is?"

Catherine answered, "Not sure, probably goat."

"Nice. Just what I always wanted to eat," Paul commented sarcastically.

After eating in silence for a couple of minutes, Paul added. "Do you think we should change our plans now that we might have someone after us?"

"We can lie low for a little while. According to the scriptures, Jesus will return and debate the Jewish leaders in the temple tomorrow. It isn't clear how much of this might happen in an area where we can observe him," Tom explained. "After that, he'll spend much of his time teaching in the temple. He'll share the Passover meal with his disciples the evening after tomorrow.

"We won't be able to observe that, but afterward, he'll go to the Garden of Gethsemane, where his arrest will happen. I think over the next two days, we should go to several of the places where He'll be going. The garden, the high priest's house, Pilate's palace, and the site of the crucifixion. When things start happening, we don't want to miss something because we get lost," Tom said.

After eating, they rested for several hours before departing again.

Chapter 41

OVER THE NEXT COUPLE OF DAYS, THE VISITORS FROM THE 21st century visited many of the key sites in the area, making sure that when the time came, they could find their way to the different important locations.

They walked through the area where the crucifixion would occur, examining the places where the view would work the best and the camera angles would have good light.

The trio headed to the Garden of Gethsemane, located on the lower slope of the Mount of Olives. They explored the area for a while and decided that in order to witness Jesus' arrest, they'd need to follow his party here. It was a massive area, so staking it out ahead of time would be impossible.

While discussing this, Paul was slammed from behind and fell down a small embankment.

Tom and Catherine spun around to see what happened and found themselves looking at the tips of short swords. Only a few inches away, the swords were held by two of the three men they'd encountered after arriving in this time period.

"We need to talk," said Daniel. "You took our property. Those blades were a gift to us, and you took them. They're important. We want them back."

"We had to steal these common ones," added Malachi. "Also, tell us what you did. How'd you do, whatever it was, to us."

Tom was concerned about Paul. The last time he'd fallen, the weight and awkwardness of the backpack unit had caused him to land poorly and break his arm. This time he went down a small rock-covered hill and, from their current location, they couldn't see where he'd landed. Still, Tom managed to compose himself enough to answer.

"We don't have your swords. We didn't keep them." As he spoke, his mind was racing. He might be able to get the taser pistol out, but it could only be fired once without taking time to reload it. Unless Catherine acted in unison with him, these guys would kill one of them easily, considering how close they were all standing.

"What did you do with them? Tell us, or we'll gut you right here!" Malachi shouted.

"We buried them near where you attacked us."

"You'll take us to them right now. Or you'll die right here. I'm supposed to be getting married tomorrow. Because of you three, I'll already be late getting back," Malachi added.

There was a sound, and everyone looked down the embankment. With his face covered in blood, Paul was coming up to the road. He'd gone down the side of the hill and was coming up at a different location than where he went down. In his hand was a metal cylinder, about half the size of a paper towel tube.

"You and your friends are going to pay for what you did. Our friend may never walk again because of his knee," Malachi said as he turned to cover Paul with his sword.

In English, Paul called out. "When I get to the road, back away quickly."

"What did you say? What language is that? What's in your hand" Malachi's questions came so fast Paul couldn't have answered, even if he'd wanted to. The man's confusion

allowed Paul to get about six feet away before Malachi realized it.

"Where are you going?" Daniel yelled at Tom and
Catherine as each took several quick steps backward.

The loud screech of agony from Malachi caused Daniel to
spin around. As Tom and Catherine continued to retreat
faster, the second spray of the CS Pepper spray hit Daniel
directly in the face, and he was on the ground shrieking with
his friend.

Paul had maneuvered so the mild breeze was to his back,
and when he attacked, it was directly blowing at the two
thugs.

Tom and Catherine worked their way back around to
Paul, avoiding the dissipating cloud of caustic chemicals.

The attackers were still rolling around on the ground,
crying, vomiting, and coughing.

Paul again gathered the attacker's swords. Catherine
almost yelled, misunderstanding Paul's intention, when he
moved toward the downed men with one of the swords
held out.

"Tom, use one of your fire starters and get a small fire
going. Catherine help me with their clothes," he instructed in
English.

In a few minutes, they'd used the sharp blades to slice all
the clothing off the still writhing men and fed them into the
fire. Gathering all the men's belongings, the trio headed back
the way they'd come, leaving their assailants still incapaci-
tated, naked, and without possessions. With a little luck, this
would keep them from being a problem for the next few
days.

Not sure why, Paul returned to one of the two men lying
on the ground and said, "None of this would have happened
if you hadn't tried to attack us. I suggest you leave us alone or
it'll be much worse next time. Go back to where you were
going to attack us. Walk towards the city for about two

minutes, then leave the road to the right. Your precious swords are buried there under some rocks."

After that, the time travelers moved a couple of hundred yards, stopped, and went to work on Paul's injuries. Fortunately, other than an inch-and-a-half laceration on the forehead, all he had were some minor bruises and abrasions.

Using a water bottle, Tom cleaned his face and applied a sterile dressing with an antibiotic cream to the head wound. Catherine then took a strip of material she'd wisely saved from the clothing they'd burned and used it to wrap Paul's head and hide the futuristic bandage.

Chapter 42

FOR THE NEXT DAY AND A HALF, THE TRIO SPENT MOST OF their time in their rented room, only occasionally venturing out for provisions or to relieve their boredom. The money given to them from the other time travelers allowed for the purchase of more bread, fruit, and smoked meat.

While resting, they reviewed some of the recordings again and were delighted with the quality.

During the second day of their quiet period, each of them tried to get as much rest as possible because the next day and a half would be hectic.

As evening approached, the team packed up all their belongings and all the food. Because it was unlikely they'd be returning to this room.

As they slipped out of the alley, Paul remembered to retrieve the motion sensor, which had fortunately remained silent, except for one occasion when their rest had been interrupted by a stray cat.

Their first destination was the Garden of Gethsemane. Upon arrival, Paul found a position where they'd be able to see anyone approaching from the city. Once Jesus and his party passed, the trio would follow at a distance. Because it was critical to be in position before Jesus and his followers arrived, they ended up lying in place for several hours.

Eventually, Jesus and his disciples arrived. Catherine counted a total of twelve men in the group. As the men passed, the three observers climbed down from the hill and followed. After about fifteen minutes, the twelve stopped, and Jesus spoke to them for a few minutes, and then he and two others continued further up the path.

The time travelers used this opportunity to advance so to where they could see clearly and hopefully hear some of what was said.

Over the next hour, things were reasonably quiet, and the nine remaining sat and rested, eventually falling asleep.

Eventually, Jesus and the two others returned and found the nine sleeping.

Even though they could see Jesus speaking to the group, the distance was too great to hear what was said clearly.

While Jesus spoke to them, a huge group moved in on him. There was one man out in front whom they'd seen with Jesus on the road and in the temple court. Behind him were some men in ornamented robes. There were many others with them, and directly behind were close to a hundred soldiers. All of them were armed, and most were carrying torches or lanterns.

Jesus and the disciples all stood and waited to face the approaching contingent.

Tom was thrilled to be here watching this. He'd heard and read this story close to a hundred times. Starting back in his Sunday school days, and here it was happening, live right in front of them.

The one in front, which everyone assumed was Judas Iscariot, walked up to Jesus and kissed him on the cheek.

Jesus spoke briefly to Judas and then addressed the men behind him. The contingent all stumbled backward as he spoke, some falling to the ground. The men arose and took a step forward, and Jesus spoke again, and they again fell back.

The next time they moved forward, one of the two men who had wandered up the trail with Jesus pulled out a sword and struck one of the official-looking men. The one he struck was standing next to one of the more richly dressed men. The blow hit him on the side of the head, and while the exact injury wasn't visible, the flowing blood was.

The observers could hear Jesus yell at the man with the sword, and he put it away. Jesus next touched the wound of the injured man, who was on his knees, and the bleeding stopped.

Jesus spoke to the group, the soldiers grabbed him, twisted his arms behind his back, bound him with a rope, and led him away.

Tom, Paul, and Catherine waited until everyone else passed their position, then fell in behind, knowing Jesus was being taken to the house of the High Priest. While the three from the future knew where to go, they still followed as close as possible in case something interesting happened which hadn't made it into the scriptures.

Chapter 43

THE CROWD WAS ALREADY GATHERING AS THE TRIO ARRIVED AT the high priest's courtyard. News of the arrest of Jesus had spread through the city. Over a hundred people were already in the courtyard, and more were arriving. It was getting cold, and several fires were burning as the people, who were trying to stay warm crowded around them.

The three outsiders tried to join in with those gathering. Everyone was talking and quite excited. Soon Catherine realized they were starting to attract attention. Their language skills weren't up to the task of fast, animated conversation. The three disengaged from the group and found themselves trying to blend into the background.

The three knew that at this time, the interrogation of Jesus by the chief priests and council would have started. Once morning came, they'd turn him over to Pilate.

As the morning approached and it was starting to become light out, everyone heard the sound of a rooster crowing. Almost immediately, a man fled past them, leaving the courtyard. He was visibly upset about something. They recognized him as Peter, who had struck with the sword in the garden.

As it became light out, Jesus was escorted from the high

priest's residence and led to the Praetorium. The Praetorium was where official Roman business took place and was also the palace where Pontius Pilate, the Roman Prefect of Judea, resided.

Many in the crowd who gathered during the night followed the procession as it moved along, escorting Jesus. While walking along, the group became more and more animated. Some instigators were walking among the people talking about all the trouble Jesus had been causing. They believed what he'd been saying had been blasphemy, and he deserved death. Soon, even the more docile members of the assembly were calling for his execution.

By the time the group reached the Praetorium, there were no longer many in the crowd sympathetic to Jesus. Many, who days ago, were praising him for the miracles he'd performed had now apparently forgotten all the amazing things he'd done. At the front of the mass of people, the Chief Priest stood, ready to testify against Jesus.

After Jesus had been inside for about two hours, a man appeared on the balcony and addressed the crowd. He was well-dressed but not in the same elaborate way the Jewish leaders had been. He seemed to have a more official presence.

When he addressed the crowd, it was in Latin rather than Hebrew or Aramaic. He spoke to the assembled. From the back of the mob, it was hard to hear what was said.

At one point, he disappeared and, after a minute, returned with Jesus, who now had on an ornamental purple robe and a crown made of twisted vines with large thorns.

When Jesus appeared, the crowd briefly grew quiet.

They could hear Pilate, say, "I'm bringing him out so you may know that I find no guilt in him."

The gathered crowd began shouting, "Crucify Him, Crucify Him!"

Pilate was visibly troubled by the conviction of the assembled. He tried to speak to them, but in the back of the crowd, the chanting drowned out what he was trying to say. Tom could only guess what was being said because he knew the scriptures. After unsuccessfully trying to convince the gathering that Jesus should be allowed to live, Pilate reluctantly surrendered Jesus to be executed.

Tom, Paul, and Catherine positioned themselves to get a good view of Jesus and were horrified by his physical condition from the severe abuse he'd suffered.

The soldiers tried to force him to carry the cross they would hang him on for his execution. It was soon apparent he wouldn't get far in his weakened condition. Slowly moving, he stumbled several times. The Roman soldiers were getting impatient with the slow progress, and they eventually grabbed a bystander and forced him to carry the cross the rest of the way.

There were mixed comments from the crowd. Many were surprised that after all Jesus had done, the Jewish leaders had turned against him. Others were disappointed because they'd believed he'd become their king. The third group was pleased with what was happening. To them, he was a fraud and troublemaker.

As the procession arrived at Golgotha, a sharp banging sound and screaming came from up ahead. Several minutes later, as those following rounded the bend, they saw the Roman soldiers raising a cross similar to the one intended for Jesus. A man was already attached to this cross, and the screaming had come from him. The soldiers stood this cross next to another, which also had a man already hanging from it. The second man was quiet and stoic, while the man being moved into place screamed curses at the soldiers.

With practiced skill, the soldiers took Jesus's cross, laid it flat, and manhandled Jesus onto it. He didn't struggle or resist.

Several soldiers used spears to keep the crowd from getting too close. Everyone seemed to crave a good view, including the three from the future, who wanted a good recording of this historical event.

Tom found himself seething with anger as he watched how his Savior was treated.

When the soldiers drove the spikes in, and Jesus screamed, all three felt sick to their stomachs. Their twenty-first-century lives weren't accustomed to such barbaric practices. The people of this time were far less impacted by what they were watching. Many of them had witnessed such savage acts before.

Once the spikes were in place, ten soldiers worked together to lift the cross.

Catherine left the others and worked her way closer. She ensured her miniature body camera pointed toward the condemned man on the cross.

As she got closer, she could hear one of the other condemned men taunting Jesus, urging him to save himself. The third hanging man rebuked him, declaring Jesus innocent and asking Jesus to remember him in heaven.

Jesus replied, "I tell you that today, you'll be with me in paradise."

As she listened, she could already hear that the men were struggling. Breathing and talking were increasingly difficult.

From her studies of the culture, Catherine was familiar with crucifixion as a form of execution. She knew the victim's death typically resulted from suffocation and heart failure. These resulted from when the body hung in that position.

The soldiers placed a sign above Jesus, and while Tom and Paul couldn't read the words, they knew exactly what it said. "JESUS OF NAZARETH, THE KING OF THE JEWS"

Several hours passed with very little spoken from the cross. Eventually, everyone who remained heard Jesus clearly say, "My God, my God, why have you forsaken me?"

Tom had known he'd hear these words as Jesus had the full wrath of God placed on him.

Knowing the end was coming, Tom moved as close as the guards would allow. Stopping only when the tip of a spear was pushed toward him, keeping him from getting any closer. He took a small step backward, showing the guard that he'd comply with the command.

Tom wanted to be there to hear the last words said. It was over a half hour, and then Jesus spoke loud but with difficulty. "Father, into your hands, I commit my spirit." Following those words, he slumped forward, and his struggles to breathe ended.

Almost instantly, there was a low rumble, the ground shook briefly, and the bright sunlight disappeared as if a thick dark cloud was blocking it. Looking up, those present saw no clouds.

Chapter 44

WHEN THE CROWD RECOVERED FROM THE STRANGE EVENTS, the trio heard some of the comments.

"Is he dead?"

"That was quicker than I expected."

"So much for him becoming king."

"I was hoping to see a miracle."

Soon many of those in attendance wandered away. Most of the crowd paid no attention to the two remaining men still lingering on their crosses. Jesus had undoubtedly been the main attraction.

Soon, after most of the people had left, the soldiers broke the legs of the two men who were crucified alongside Jesus because they hadn't died yet.

Breaking the legs was done to speed up their deaths. With the legs broken, the condemned could no longer use their legs to push their bodies upwards. Raising up took the stress off their chests and allowed them to breathe. When the legs were broken, death from suffocation came much quicker.

The soldiers were prepared to break the legs of Jesus but didn't bother once they noticed he was already dead. Instead, one of the soldiers jabbed him in the left side of his chest with a spear. Clear fluid and blood ran from the wound. Tom noticed the spear which pierced Jesus was the same one a soldier recently used to prevent himself from getting closer to the Cross. He wasn't sure why, but he found it mildly exciting.

When the crucifixion was complete, the soldiers waved two men forward. These men had stood alongside two women who had been actively crying throughout the entire event. These men came forward with a small ladder. They climbed the back of the cross using the ladder, took a long linen cloth, looped it under Jesus' armpits, and then up over the cross's horizontal bar. While one of them held the linen, the other used a hammer and knocked the nails holding Jesus out from the back of the cross. The men then gently used the linen strap to gently lower Jesus' body to the ground.

The two women met them at the foot of the cross, and together they carefully wrapped the body in preparation for burial.

Chapter 45

As Jesus' body was carried away, several groups followed. There were a handful of his followers and friends who had remained. There were also half a dozen soldiers, followed by some of the religious leaders. Finally, there were three simply dressed people from two thousand years in the future.

Paul, Tom, and Catherine followed at a distance, stopping frequently to make sure they stayed as far back as possible. For once, the trio wasn't as interested in being close to the action as they were in being inconspicuous.

When the procession eventually stopped at a small opening in the rock-faced hill, Paul led them for about fifty yards before stopping to observe. The two men and two women took the body in through the gap in the rock, then headed back the way they'd come.

The soldier who appeared to be in charge stepped into the tomb and returned after less than a minute, having assured all was in order. Two other soldiers took positions on either side of the opening while the others worked to roll a massive stone into place to block the entrance completely. Once the stone was in place, the soldiers stretched a string across it and secured it on either side. This official Roman seal would show if the tomb was tampered with.

When this was complete, Paul, Tom, and Catherine continued further down the road before leaving the trail and heading out into the rough terrain.

Once the trio was far enough away that they couldn't be seen, the time travelers sat and prepared supper. The meal consisted of dehydrated beef stew, which was heated over a fire they started with a Trioxane fuel tablet. Trioxane is a chemical fuel that burns quite hot, makes no smoke, leaves no ash behind, and each of the team members carried several packets.

"That was far more barbaric than I was expecting. I almost threw up when the nails were going in," Paul admitted as he started eating.

"I had studied this culture and time frame for years, but being here and seeing it in person is completely different," Catherine added.

They both waited for Tom to comment, but he remained silent.

Finally, Catherine said, "Tom?"

"I don't know how I feel. You see, for a Christian, his death on the cross is my redemption. My one path to heaven. It was both the most horrible and most wonderful thing I've ever seen. I was furious and disgusted by what I saw, but also so thankful at the same time," Tom said.

The team sat in silence and ate for a while. Then Tom said in a more light-hearted voice. "Paul, do you still think you might win this wager?"

Paul grinned and replied. "Ever since he healed my arm, I've known I wouldn't win. I'll be shocked if we see anything other than him walking from the tomb."

"Yea, I think you might lose Paul. However, I'm not fully convinced yet. I want to see what happens in a few days," Catherine added.

After eating and cleaning up, they waited for dark. Then they slowly advanced, well off the road, towards the tomb. The trio stopped about one hundred yards away. Paul and Tom worked quietly, moving rocks and stacking them.

They created a concealed position where one person could lie and observe with small binoculars and a video camera with a long-distance lens. The forward position was then covered with camouflage netting, and secured in place with rocks. This location was close enough to see everything that happened and be completely hidden.

While Paul settled into position, Tom and Catherine moved back about fifty yards and set up a second area. This location is where two of them would eat, sleep and wait for their turn to the observation position.

The three of them decided that three hours in the forward position and six eating and resting would be a good rotation.

Tom unrolled three solar collectors. Each, when unfolded, was the size of a hand towel. The collectors would be used to charge some of the depleted batteries from the video cameras. They were rapidly going through their battery supply, and this would extend their capacity.

Once everything was in place, Tom and Catherine helped each other remove their packs. It felt great to have them off after almost twenty-four hours with them on continuously. Paul would keep his pack on until it was his turn to rest.

Tom inspected the packs, looking for any signs of damage, and checked battery levels, which were at about twenty-seven percent. The power levels were lower than they'd hoped but still enough to get them home in two days. Checking the diagnostic panel, he saw all twelve LEDs were green, indicating there were no mechanical problems.

Chapter 46

WHILE HIS TEAMMATES RESTED, PAUL VERIFIED THE VIDEO recorder was working. He ran the camera for a few minutes, then stopped and checked the quality of the recording and was delighted. Even in the low light of night, the camera was picking up considerable detail. He could easily see the guard and the stone sealing the tomb and could even see him speaking to someone who had walked past.

Even though the resurrection was two days away, the team recorded the tomb constantly. If someone stole Jesus's body instead of it being resurrected, they needed to record that critical event. However, as Paul lay here, he began to think someone stealing the body was more and more unlikely to happen.

Paul reminded himself this whole adventure wasn't about the wager but about proving and demonstrating this fantastic ability to go back in time. As he lay still, with the binoculars propped on a rock, he wished they'd thought to bring one of the sleeping mats here. The ground was extremely rocky, and lying here wasn't pleasant. This would be a long three-hour shift, and he'd have several more over the next two days.

Two hours into Paul's first shift, about twenty men

approached the soldier. There was a bit of a verbal dispute, and Paul started to wonder if these men might be here to take the body. However, the confrontation ended almost as quickly as it started, and the men returned the way they'd come.

As he continued to lie on the ground observing, his mind wandered. He allowed himself to consider some troubling events. These thoughts he'd intentionally been pushing aside until now. First, there was the way trusted members of his team had, without authorization, used the time-traveling process for their personal benefit. Even more disturbing was how they managed to do it without being discovered. Going forward, how would he control this? Just as distressing was the idea that a simple interaction like staying the night in the wrong place could be so devastating to the future. For the first time, Paul started to doubt if there would ever be a way to show the world what they'd invented.

As his shift ended, Paul was aware no sounds were coming from Tom or Catherine and assumed they were asleep. He decided he'd let them sleep another hour if one of them didn't come to relieve him. He was exhausted but could hold out a little longer. Picking up the binoculars, he took another close look at the soldiers and confirmed there was no one else around.

As he set them down, he heard a faint noise and then felt the presence of someone next to him. He slid backward from the enclosure he had built and was assisted to his feet by Tom.

Whispering, Tom said, "My turn. Anything interesting?"

"You were very quiet; I thought you were still asleep."

"I wish. That wasn't long enough of a rest. The worst part was having to put this pack back on," Tom stated.

"I bet. I'm going to get mine off and go to sleep."

Paul then described the confrontation between the soldiers and the group an hour before. Wanting Tom to be aware in case the men returned.

Paul then left the observation point and retreated to where

Catherine was. After removing the pack, he ate some dried fruit. After that, he was soon asleep and didn't awaken for six hours when he had to return and relieve Catherine at the observation post.

Chapter 47

THE TWO-AND-A-HALF DAYS OF WATCHING AND WAITING WERE monotonous and seemed to drag on forever. The only excitement came the first morning when Catherine, who was sound asleep, awoke to a large dog standing over her. It was tan with a single black ear and snout. She almost screamed but caught herself.

"Hello there. Are you friendly?" She asked in as calm a tone as she could. As she spoke, her hand was working its way toward the taser. At about the same time she got her hand around it, the dog curled up and lay down, leaning against her thigh, with his tail repeatedly smacking the ground next to her. She released her grip on the weapon and started stroking the thick fur on his neck.

He remained with them for the remainder of their visit to this time period. All three enjoyed his company, even though he ate some of their food. It turned out none of them minded sharing with him. They had enough, and his presence was comforting. Tom started calling him Quantum, saying he needed to have a name.

The following night at midnight, they were all awake and

lying on their bellies at the forward observation post, to be able to view what would happen at the critical moment.

Suddenly Quantum started whining and getting anxious. Catherine placed a hand on him, and he quieted down. Immediately after the dog started getting excited, two small dots of light appeared directly in front of the tomb. The dots rapidly grew in size and formed into the shape of cloaked men. They glowed bright white and were easily seven feet tall or more. As soon as these newcomers appeared, the guard fled.

Once fully formed, their blinding glow dimmed considerably, but they still radiated light.

The two focused on the stone, and one of them raised a hand and swept it from left to right, and the stone rolled away without being touched.

Only a second or two after the stone was gone, there was another blinding light. This one came from within the tomb. It remained for about five seconds and then was gone.

The two cloaked figures removed their hoods and knelt on the ground with their heads bowed. A minute later, someone walked out from the tomb. It was clear it was the risen Jesus. Approaching the two angelic beings, he placed a hand on each, and they stood. He spoke to them for about a minute. While completing his discussion, he pointed out into the desert directly at the observation post. The huge men turned, looked where Jesus was pointing, and nodded. Jesus said a few more words, then he turned and walked away.

The angels transformed back into the hot white light and disappeared.

Tom, Catherine, and Paul watched the tomb for several minutes and then withdrew to their resting spot.

"That was amazing!" Catherine said.

"I agree! I didn't know what to expect, but that was incredible!" Paul added.

Tom didn't speak; he simply stood thinking about what

he'd witnessed.

"Well, Tom, you certainly won the wager," Catherine announced.

Tom nodded, seeming distracted.

"Tom, is there a problem?" Paul asked.

Finally, he spoke. "We just witnessed mighty angels drop to their knees and bow their heads in respect to the Lord. The whole time we were spying on them. I kinda feel guilty. I certainly am amazed by what we saw, but it also feels wrong. It's like a kid peeking in someone's window and seeing something that should have been private."

They all stood silently for almost half a minute before Tom spoke again. "What do you think it meant when He pointed at us, and the others nodded?"

Catherine replied, "I don't know about you, but it made me a bit uncomfortable."

"Yeah, it sure looked like they were talking about us," Paul remarked.

"Tom, do you think we need to observe anything else before heading back? The batteries in the systems are getting low, but we could remain about another half day," Paul asked.

"The women will come and find the tomb empty, and then Jesus will speak to them. Then Peter will come and also see the empty tomb. But I think we've done what we came here to do. I think it is time for us to go home."

After agreeing, it took less than ten minutes to pack all their equipment and remove all signs of their having been there.

All three were now wearing their packs and inspected them again to ensure everything was in working order.

Catherine said goodbye to her big canine friend, and then they stood together.

Paul spoke, "On three, one, two, and three."

They all pressed the recessed button on the bottom of their backs and disappeared.

Chapter 48

In the blink of an eye, Tom and Paul appeared in the lab. There was immediate applause from those gathered around. Linda, Michelle, and much of the staff rushed forward.

"You're back? But you just left," Linda said.

Shocked, Paul called out, "Where is Catherine?"

No sooner was the question out than he felt an intense pain in his right calf and glanced down and realized Tom had kicked him quite hard. Tom glared at him and shook his head.

"What did you say?" Several people asked, not hearing well over all the commotion.

"Paul! What happened to your head?" Michelle all but shouted.

At the same time, Linda asked, "Did you see him? Did you see Jesus?"

"Easy! One at a time. Tom called out."

Everyone paused and then wanted to see what was wrong with Paul's head. The large laceration was scabbed over but still impressive.

Paul responded. "We can look at that later. It happened four days ago. The day before the crucifixion."

Linda was the first to respond. "Did you see it? Witnessed the whole thing?"

"Yes, all of it," Paul said. "We'll explain everything. Just give us a couple of minutes to get this equipment off and clean up. All I'll say now is it's official. I lost the wager."

Linda shouted with joy, and Michelle smiled and nodded. She might not have been overly religious, but she wasn't surprised to hear how this turned out.

Staff from the lab got through the excited family members and assisted with safely removing the backpacks and disabling the thermite charges.

The packs got plugged into computer stations, and their data was downloaded. The men surrendered their audio and video recording equipment, cameras, and the filled data drives. Altogether these devices held several terabytes of recordings. As the data was turned in, each audio and video device was labeled as to who it came from, and each drive was logged in the order in which the recordings were made.

Once all the equipment was taken care of, Paul again addressed the group. "Please give us a few minutes. We haven't showered in almost three weeks. Linda, and Michelle, please place a delivery order; we need food." Everyone laughed at that statement. Pausing, he looked at the staff and continued. "We'll all meet in the conference room in twenty minutes and tell you everything and review some of the videos."

They descended into the basement and entered one of the small meeting rooms at the base of the stairs.

"She is gone! We have to get her back!" Paul said adamantly.

"Calm down, Paul. We need to figure out what happened and if there's anything we can do," Tom explained as he logged into a computer.

"You knew this was going to happen? You understood as soon as we got here," Paul said, the confusion evident in his voice.

"I suspected it was possible. Based on what the two from the future said and how they reacted to her, I was afraid this might happen. There was nothing we could do back there, so I hoped I was wrong," Tom explained.

Looking up from the computer, Tom added, "I just reviewed the facility directory for the university. Catherine isn't listed. Her social media accounts don't exist."

Paul sat on a table and shook his head, "We have to do something. It's like she never existed."

Tom nodded, "She never did exist, not in this timeline. Something we did back there wiped her family line from history."

Still stunned, Paul said, "What can we do?"

"First, I'm not sure what we can do. In our current reality, Catherine never existed. If we go back and warn ourselves, it won't make any sense because she never existed to them. Also, remember this isn't urgent. We can correct this anytime, if possible. We need time to think. Let's get cleaned up and go back upstairs and show everyone what we learned. Try not to let on that something is wrong."

Leaving the room, the men went to the locker rooms that were available to all the staff before and after work and during lunch.

Retrieving the bags with the clothes they'd arrived in before their trip, the two headed to the showers.

The uncomfortable, filthy, stinking, and in some cases, bloody clothes came off and went into trash bags. Michelle had suggested keeping them because a display of artifacts from their first actual time-traveling adventure might be interesting.

The hot water felt amazing, and the shampoo in the hair was almost as welcome.

Once finished, the clean clothes and deodorant were a welcome change from what they'd worn for most of the last week.

Chapter 49

It had been almost twenty minutes when the three entered the conference room, and it would be another fifteen before the twelve pizzas arrived. There was much animated talking taking place as the men arrived.

Michelle was the first to speak to them. "Paul, I think you forgot something," everyone laughed. They all saw Tom's face, cleanly shaved for the first time in many months, and Paul's, which still had a long wild beard.

"I was thinking of keeping it."

"Not if you're coming home with me," Michelle added.

This comment generated more laughter from the group.

Everyone got quiet when Paul brought up the laptop and the first video.

"This footage is still raw. When we get it cleaned up, we'll have a more detailed showing, but for now, we'll show a few highlights. These images are from the body camera I was wearing," Paul explained.

The scene started when they first arrived.

Tom began discussing the culture and how the people acted towards them, then rushed ahead, skipping to the first attack and then to how Paul broke his arm. These two topics caused quite a bit of discussion. Much of the video of both events was a bit distorted because of all the movement of the body cameras.

Tom explained that they could splice together something much better when both sets of videos were edited and cleaned up

Both men noticed how Catherine was eerily absent from all the videos.

Paul next skipped ahead to when Jesus spoke to them.

Seeing Jesus on the video was incredible; everyone gasped when he spoke English. As he walked away and Paul exclaimed how his arm was healed, the whole room was on their feet staring at the screen.

Paul stopped the video and let the many discussions in the room continue. Knowing how amazed he'd felt then and still felt seeing it again, he understood the need for the group to discuss this.

After a few minutes, Paul said. "We're all getting a little tired, and work still needs to be done. I'm going to forward to the most exciting part."

Paul again changed the data drives and inserted the one from the video camera used at the tomb. Fast forwarding the video, he stopped to give everyone some background on where they were and how long they'd been waiting.

The image started moving, and the tomb was quite visible even though it was nighttime. After about a minute, everyone could hear the sound of a dog whining and getting excited. Then the video went completely white. All pictures and sound were gone, but according to the computer, there were still several minutes left. Everyone waited, hoping the image would return, but it never did.

Paul raced from the room and headed to the lab. Hoping one of the body cameras would have captured the resurrection.

While he was gone, Tom described in detail what

happened at the tomb. It was then that the food arrived, and everyone started passing the pizzas around.

When Paul returned, he had the data drives from both body cameras, connected them to the computer, one at a time, and played the video watching the timestamp in the bottom corner. In each case, the video went all white at precisely the same time, and the audio stopped picking anything up.

Chapter 50

Several days later, Paul and Tom sat together talking.

"I still don't understand. The camera is working fine now; we've checked all the recordings. Why is it that only that specific period of time is missing?" Paul grumbled.

"First, what are the chances all the cameras which worked flawlessly for days and are fine now all failed at precisely the same time?" Tom asked.

"It would be impossible on their own unless they were acted upon by an outside force," Paul admitted.

"This is what I was talking about months ago when I said I was a little uncomfortable trying to prove to the world that the resurrection occurred. Remember, I said faith is one of the crucial parts of Christianity. Faith in God, in Jesus, and in his Bible. That means faith in his ability to save and in his resurrection is needed. Truly proving it means there's no need for faith anymore. If we were to prove the resurrection to the world, we'd mess up God's plan for salvation and what He went to the cross for," Tom explained.

"So, are you saying Jesus prevented us from recording the resurrection?" Paul asked.

"That is what I think happened. Either that or Jesus had it

erased afterward. Remember him pointing us out to the angels?"

"I'm not sure how to feel about this," Paul admitted.

"We still accomplished our primary mission. We have the information we need to show a major scientific breakthrough, the ability to travel back in time. Also, we all have seen the proof of the resurrection. For us, there's no longer any question of that," Tom explained.

"That's my bigger dilemma," Paul said. "Should we announce this at all? In the short time this technology has existed, we've seen significant problems. Two people that we're aware of from our own team attempted to use it for improper personal gain. One is dead or, at the least, trapped in the past. We had to be intercepted by people from the future to keep us from causing a disaster by simply sleeping in the wrong place.

"That is one thing I still can't stop thinking about. We also know, from our friends from the future, that there were other changes to the lives of others for thousands of years, which weren't as significant. Then, of course, there's Catherine. We recruited her and somehow changed things so she no longer exists. She was one of us, and somehow we accidentally deleted her family line."

"Are you thinking that this technology should remain secret?" Tom inquired.

"We need to think long and hard about who we tell and how much access we allow to it."

They sat in silence for a while, disappointed but entirely in agreement. Time travel was a desirable and valuable technology, but it was also extremely dangerous.

Finally, Paul got a grin on his face. "I know one thing for sure; we'll join you in church this Sunday."

Chapter 51

IT WAS TWO MONTHS AFTER THE FANTASTIC ADVENTURE BACK in time, and Paul and Michelle stood side by side. Paul was exhausted from another sleepless night, and Michelle felt as drained.

Paul had been turning his problems over and over in his mind, day and night, since returning. How to get Catherine back, & how to prevent this amazing technology from being misused? Those questions always led to another. Who is to say what an appropriate use of time travel would be? Was going back in time to save Tom's mother as wrong as what Charlie and Bruce did?

And there was still Bruce. He'd promised to help him reverse his wife's death months ago and still hadn't followed through. But that promise was always secondary, and now with Catherine gone, it was an even lower concern.

Paul knew the visit from the two from the future was another major issue he wrestled with. They'd shown him the real danger of being able to change time inadvertently. There was a solution, but it was so radical he'd not been ready to accept it until recently. Getting Michelle to agree took even longer.

When the music stopped, the Pastor stood, and as usual, he concluded the service with a prayer.

As everyone began to leave, Tom glanced at Paul and Michelle. "Are you two okay? You both were quiet before the service and seemed distracted after it started."

"Yea, we're okay. We just have some stuff on our minds," Paul explained.

"No problem," Michelle added with a reassuring smile which to Tom felt forced.

"Do you two want to join us for lunch? We're going for Chinese. We have to get the kids from their classes, but are going after that." Linda asked.

"Maybe next time. We need to take care of some things today," Michelle responded.

Following the brief conversation, Paul and Michelle exited the sanctuary and went to the parking lot. The pair intentionally avoided some of the people they'd started getting to know in the last couple of months.

Once safely in their vehicle, Paul said, "You okay?"

Michelle nodded, "Let's go."

The drive was in silence, neither of them wanting to speak. They made one quick stop at a grocery store at Michelle's insistence, and then after almost fifteen minutes, arrived at the Kingsman Research Institute.

Entering the Institute, the couple passed through the lobby and headed upstairs. As Paul stepped off the escalator, someone suddenly stood about ten feet in front of him. One moment there was no one there, and the next, a man was standing in front of him. He was somewhat tall and dressed all in white. The electronic device was visible, encircling his right wrist.

Paul recognized him, but not before the man's sudden appearance caused both him and Michelle to gasp.

"Mr. Kingsman, Mrs. Kingsman. Or are you still Mrs. Rogers?" the man said, smiling at the couple.

"Michelle Rogers," she clarified.

"Sorry. I should have made sure to have that detail."

"I had a feeling we might be seeing you. Where's your partner?" Paul asked.

"Protocol dictates they only send one of us if we aren't trying to conceal who we are. There's less chance of contaminating the timeline that way. We need to talk about what you're planning. We think you are about to create a deviation from the original timeline. Something has caused a change that put you on an alternate path."

"Your interaction with us was what convinced me. You're the cause of the deviation. This needs to be done. Lives have been forever changed, and many more will be over the years," Paul explained.

"That's true, but your actions will dramatically alter your future and my past."

"I am preventing my invention from disrupting the future by removing it from existence. Tell me, in your year, how many people's lives in your past have been changed by my invention?

"Tens of thousands, possibly hundreds of thousands," the visitor from the future admitted.

"That's why I must do this. The consequences of my work are too great. I need to stop it before it ever happens," Paul explained.

"I'll inform our committee of your plans. They'll decide if we'll allow this," as he spoke, he pressed a button on the wide band on his wrist and disappeared.

Michelle took hold of Paul's arm. "Can he stop us?"

"If his people want to stop us, I'm sure they can. Any minute he could return. Maybe with others and force us to stop."

The couple walked to Paul's office, and he went to his chair and sat. He worked quickly, powering on the two laptops and handing one to Michelle. Each confirmed all the needed files were in place. They gathered documents, photos, and some other items Paul had set aside the day before. These were placed along with the laptops, and chargers into two identical black nylon backpacks.

Taking the packs, they went to the lab. Once there, Paul got two of the bulky backpack units and moved them to the workbench. With Michelle watching, he hooked up the power and data lines and went to work on the computer. He programmed in all the data about dates and locations, and the systems went to work calculating the formulas.

As the system worked, the loving couple sat together, holding hands. "I need to ask again. Will it really be us?" Michelle asked as a tear ran down her cheek.

"Yes, it will."

"And we'll be together again?"

"If we do this right, we'll be together," Paul replied, trying to comfort her.

Finally, the computer reported that the matrix was complete. Paul checked the indicator lights on the backpacks and saw they were all green.

After disconnecting the power and data lines from the first one, he assisted Michelle in putting it on. Next, he handed her one of the black backpacks. She added the bag she got from the store to hers, then he kissed her and said, "I love you."

She smiled, closed her eyes, and took a couple of deep breaths to compose herself. Her expression changed from sorrow to focused determination. She pressed the button and disappeared.

Paul picked up his pack and got his arms through the straps. After disconnecting the cables running to the pack, he grabbed the laptop case.

Paul thought of how at the least, he was about to fulfill his part of the wager, even if it wasn't in the way any of them had ever imagined.

Taking a moment to reexamine what he was about to do,

he closed his eyes. When he opened them, he pressed the button.

He was in the lab one moment, and the next, he was in a familiar apartment that he'd not seen in about twenty years.

The only other person in the apartment sat on the couch, and he jumped to his feet as the man with the strange backpack appeared in front of him.

"What? Who are you? How did you do that?" he blurted out.

Paul smiled at his younger self.

"Relax. If I'm correct, your fiancée, Maureen, is out of town for a few days visiting her parents, and you don't have to be back to class until the day after tomorrow. We have lots of time to talk."

Chapter 52

463 YEARS IN THE FUTURE

THE CONTROL ROOM WAS ABOUT THE SIZE OF A BASKETBALL court. There were massive display screens on all the walls. Operators sat in chairs that hovered in places around the room and were reclined to various degrees. Each chair was perfectly conformed to the body of the person seated in it. An arm was attached to the chairs, which displayed a holographic control panel that changed as the operator needed. There were currently four operators on duty. They each wore a headset to communicate with each other or the agents in the separate room.

The operators were aware there was increased excitement today. In the last hour, several committee members had appeared in the teleportation chamber and headed directly into the sizable conference room. There was a change to the timeline, which had everyone worked up.

"I don't understand the urgency. We aren't constrained by time. We can intervene later if the timeline is altered. That's how it has always been explained to me," Malcolm stated. He was the center's director and was the latest to arrive in the room, which overlooked the control room. All but one of the committee members was now present.

A short, lean man named Lou answered. "Normally, that's correct. However, in this case, Kingsman traveled twenty years into his past and met with his former self. We suspect he will alter his future, either by speeding up his development of time travel technology or preventing it altogether. Suppose this change to the timeline prevents the development of his quantum matrix. In that case, time travel technology may never exist or will be delayed by decades or centuries."

Gesturing toward the wide window overlooking the control room. Lou continued, "None of this will exist in our timeline because the committee will never be needed. We won't be responsible for protecting the timeline. No one will need to be. In that reality, who knows what we'll be doing, but it won't be this."

"How long do we've to stop him?" Malcolm asked.

Suddenly another person appeared in the middle of the room. Like most of the others, he wore all white. "If we decide to stop him, we don't have long. He's planning to prevent the creation of time travel technology. I just spoke to him," said the new arrival, who was tall with short-cropped hair and was Lou's immediate supervisor.

"In the time period he traveled to, he's meeting with himself. If he succeeds in convincing his former self not to develop the quantum matrix. If that occurs, all this stops existing everywhere because it never happened," Lou elaborated.

"You said if we stop him. Are you suggesting we don't go back in time and preserve the quantum matrix? That will mean it's never developed? Isn't stopping changes to the time-line what we're here for?" Asked Malcolm.

"Kingsman created the matrix, and ever since, there have been hundreds of minor changes to the timeline, and some major ones. We have reversed most of the major ones, but all the minor ones still have an impact. Many people, with no major impact on civilization, have either not been born or were created by the changes. We cannot reverse them all. At one time, it was proposed to go back and stop Kingsman before he developed his matrix. Now it looks like he's doing that for us," continued the supervisor.

"Countless amounts of time, effort, and money have gone into managing the damage from time travel over the years. Who knows what could be accomplished if those resources were redirected elsewhere? If we do nothing and let Kingsman proceed, that'll happen," Lou added.

Everyone got very quiet. There was enormous implication with either direction.

"Exactly what is meant by a minor change that wasn't prevented? Can you give me an example?" One of the other committee members asked.

"When Lou and I went back and interacted with Kingsman before the resurrection of Christ. There was a woman on his team named Catherine Collins. History shows she never existed. His team did something that kept her from ever being born. Probably just a small interaction that seemed insignificant at the time. There was no significant disruption in the events that followed, so protocol says we didn't try to correct that small error," explained the supervisor.

"How can a change which causes someone who should have lived, to never be born, be considered insignificant?"

"Even our trained agents can inadvertently cause a change when we go back to correct something, as we're seeing with Kingsman now. If we went back for every minor change to the timeline, we'd probably do as much harm as good. Therefore the protocols dictate there has to be a significant change to a large number of people, historical events, or an entire society for us to risk going back to correct it."

"Over the years, how many of these minor events have there been?"

The supervisor looked at Lou, who answered, "We have

documented two hundred and six. There were seventeen in Kingsman's trip back to biblical times alone."

"Since the change of one life will impact future generations, how many lives have been impacted?"

"We don't have an exact number, but we estimate it is close to a hundred and sixteen thousand," Lou explained.

"A hundred and sixteen thousand! All those lives were created or prevented because time travel was invented by Kingsman over four hundred years ago," Malcolm commented.

"We can undo all of that if we do nothing and allow Kingsman to complete his mission and remove his technology from existence," The supervisor stated.

"At least until someone else invents it," Lou added.

"Ok, I vote we do nothing. Let Paul Kingsman change history and reverse all the damage," declared Malcolm.

The others all somberly nodded their heads in agreement.

Chapter 53

MICHELLE ROGERS GOT OUT OF HER CAR AND HEADED INSIDE the house. Even though it was only 4:14 PM, she was ready to go to bed and cry herself to sleep. That was her routine for the last couple of weeks, ever since her husband had left after telling her she was defective.

She entered the home, which held too many memories of her marriage, and her tears started again. Besides sorrow, she was also disgusted with herself. She knew her personal situation was impacting her students. The kids might only be teenagers, but they could sense something was wrong with their teacher. Several had tried to talk to her, but she brushed their attempts off.

Still, she was sorry this was a Friday. The weekend would be terrible without the distraction of work to somewhat take her mind off her situation.

She went to the kitchen, looked in the freezer, and saw two small boxes. Without reading what the packages contained, she took out one of the frozen dinners and tossed it in the microwave.

When the food was heated, she transferred it to a plate, headed to the living room, and sat on the couch. She took the remote and turned on the TV, hoping for a distraction as she ate.

Without warning, someone was blocking her view of the TV. It was a woman in blue jeans and a sweatshirt. The sweatshirt had the logo of the high school Michelle taught at. The woman was holding a black backpack and wore an odd-looking metal backpack.

For some reason, the idea of two backpacks was the part Michelle focused on.

Looking up, she was shocked to see the intruder's face. This woman could be her twin. She was wearing her hair down, and it was a bit ruffled looking, not the way Michelle ever wore it, but other than that, she was almost identical, though maybe a few years older.

Without a word, the new arrival opened the nylon backpack, took out a grocery bag, and tossed it to her.

Catching it, Michelle noticed it was cold. She glanced inside and saw gourmet strawberry ice cream.

"Who are you, and what's with the ice cream? And how did you get in here?"

The woman smiled, "You'll soon fall in love with that kind, and we'll eat lots of it over the next few months. It helped me through your breakup when I went through it."

Michelle stared at the woman; what she said didn't make much sense, but the voice and smile were equal to her own.

"Again, who are you, and what's that thing you are wearing?"

As the woman worked to take the heavy device off her back, she said, "You already know who I am. I'm you from several years in the future. I'll help you through this time and prepare you for what's to come. And trust me; there's someone much better out there waiting for you; his name is Paul."

Epilogue

PAUL KINGSMAN SAT AT HIS DESK AND LOOKED AT THE CLOCK
on his computer as he'd already done over twenty times today.
He was feeling anxious and a little frightened. He'd been
secretly looking forward to this date for almost twenty years,
ever since the crazy Saturday when his entire life changed.
The day he came face to face with himself.

Since that day, he'd been running an almost scripted existence, following the path he and his future self mapped out
during their two days together.

After today, he had one final act to perform, and then he'd
be off on his own without any further guidance. In eighteen
months, on February third, he had to go to Tom's mother's
house early on a snowy morning and shovel her front steps. It
was a one-time thing on a specific day. That was the strangest
of all the things his future self told him to do.

Again he thought about all he'd learned from his older
self. The financial advice he got from his counterpart allowed
him the build and run the Kingsman Institute. He'd provided
himself with insight on what stocks to buy and when.

The purchase of over 4000 bitcoin back when he could

get them for five cents each and later sold them for nearly $15,000 each added to the wealth.

However, he also thought about what he'd voluntarily given up. The ability to travel in time. A knowledge that he'd once developed and now never would. He trusted it was for the best, but he'd still love to be able to go back in time, just once.

Most of all, he thought about what his former self had taught him about Jesus and how science didn't have to clash with scripture. He'd come to know Christ over eighteen years earlier than his other self and was extremely grateful. That alone was worth all he lost.

He got up from his desk to leave his office and, as was his habit, brushed his hand over the well-worn Bible he kept on his desk.

Stopping in the adjoining office, he saw Tom Wallace working at his computer.

"Tom, I need to deal with something. I'll see you in the morning."

"Ok, see you then," said Tom looking up from his work.

Paul headed down the hall toward the escalator. As he approached, he heard a female voice speaking, and with a smile, he walked to the railing which overlooked the foyer below. He often stood here and listened as the guides started their tours. Paul had led more than a few tours in the earlier years and was happy the company was now big enough to have someone else do that job.

Listening as she spoke, he heard, "The mission of the Kingsman Institute is to use modern science to prove the existence of God. Many nowadays think scientific discovery removes God from the discussion. But that isn't true; here, we use the advanced scientific discoveries to prove there had to be a creator involved."

Paul would have enjoyed staying and listening longer, but

his timing was critical. He hurried down the escalator and out of the building. In moments he was headed into town.

The drive took ten minutes, but traffic was light, and he arrived at his destination with time to spare. Stopping in the parking lot of a fast-food restaurant, he waited with the vehicle in gear and ready. As he waited, he felt his hands sweating and his heart racing. He'd considered several spots along this section of roadway, but this parking lot gave him excellent visibility and the ability to pull out quickly. Paul took a minute to pray. He'd been assured this would work but he still felt uneasy.

After almost ten minutes of waiting, he saw what he was looking for. An old blue Volkswagen Bug was approaching.

Needing to guarantee he ended up directly in front of that car, he also had to make sure not to spook the driver into changing lanes by pulling out too quickly.

Paul pulled out into traffic and tried to maintain an average speed, even though nothing about what he was doing was ordinary. Driving on, he fought to keep the Volkswagen about a single vehicle distance behind him.

There was an intersection ahead, and the light was green, so he slowed his approach a little. He needed to bring the Bug a little closer. He was almost at the traffic light now, and it turned yellow.

At this distance, Paul thought it was a tossup as to whether he'd usually stop or go, however, today, there was only one choice, and he stopped his vehicle.

Paul's eyes stayed on the rear-view mirror and watched as the bug tried to stop but couldn't and hit him from behind, as he knew it would.

Paul felt the seatbelt dig into his shoulder and mild pain in his back from the minor impact. After a few seconds, he opened the door and carefully stood. He looked back and saw a relatively attractive woman getting out of the car. She was rubbing a sore spot on her forehead.

They slowly approached each other and, in a voice that cracked as he spoke, said. "I take it you're Michelle?"

Anxiously nodding her head, she replied, "Paul?"

"I have been waiting to meet you for almost twenty years."

About the Author

 Christopher Coates writes action / adventure / sci-fi novels. Having spent 30 years in Fire / EMS and an overlapping 20 years in Information Systems, his books tend to have the occasional integration of medicine and technology.

Christopher grew up in Cape Cod, Massachusetts, and moved to Michigan to attend Davenport University. He currently lives in Kent City, Michigan, with his wife, 2 grown kids, and their 2 dogs.

———

To learn more about Christopher Coates and discover more Next Chapter authors, visit our website at www.nextchapter.pub.